Shell Windows
Short Stories from Goa

BROADWAY
PUBLISHING HOUSE

Shell Windows - Short Stories from Goa
Copyright © Fundação Oriente - Goa

Published by:

175, Filipe Neri Xavier Road,
Fontainhas, Panjim, Goa 403 001.
Tel: 0832 2230728, 2436108
Email: foriente@dataone.in

&

BROADWAY PUBLISHING HOUSE

SIGNATURE STORE:
1st Floor, Ashirwad Bldg.,Near Caculo Island,
18th June Road,Panjim-Goa.
Tel: 2420677, 6647037, 6647038, Fax: 6647038
Website: *www.bbcbooks.net* Email:*bbcbooks@rediffmail.com*

CACULO MALL:
Caculo Enclave, St. Inez, Panaji - Goa. Tel: 2233338/9

MARGAO:
Paulino Building, Ground Floor, Near Popular High School,
Comba, Margao-Goa. Tel: 6489777, (M) 9860030339

CANDOLIM:
Landscape Holiday Unit, Ground Floor, Near Dr. Dukle's Hospital &
Research Centre, Aguada Fort Road, Candolim-Goa.
Tel: 6519777, (M) 9860030339

DUBAI:
Shop No.19, A1 Wahda Bldg., Opp. Deira City Centre Metro Stn.
Port Saeed, Deira, P.O. Box: 211373,
Tel: +971 4 2500688, (M) +971 558728529
E-mail: *info@booksindubai.com*

All rights to the stories are held by the individual authors. No parts of this work may be reproduced, stored in a retrieval system or transmitted in any form or by any means, electronic, mechanical, photocopying, recording or otherwise without prior written permission of the copyright owner.

ISBN NO.: 978-93-80837-83-3   Price: 195 /-

Cover design by Conrad Pinto
Cover photographs by Willy Goes
Printed by Rama Harmalkar 9326102225

for all those who gaze
upon shells and seek
their stories

Contents

Introduction	vii
Mr Secondhand *Manohar Shetty*	1
Mushrooms *Hemant Aiya*	9
Angel *Roxanna Pinto*	17
The Dead Donkey *Pralay Bakshi*	24
Pause *Nayana Adarkar*	31
Son of the Soil *Nikhil Ribeiro*	38
The Blessed Man *Kiran Mahambre*	49
Tulsi and Tessika *Ahmed Bunglowala*	54

The Little Pink Purse — 63
Giselda Menezes

The Legend of the Rakhonddar — 72
Celina Amaral e Cota

The Girl in the Frame — 78
Aldina Braganza e Gomes

Them Bones — 89
Tanvi Srivastava

The Transformation — 96
Prashanti Talpankar

The Return — 106
Belinda Viegas

Neruda in November — 113
Marilia Fernandes

Paradise of Fools — 122
Ramnath Gawde

The Homecoming — 135
Cordelia Francis

Not So Feeble — 145
Bevinda Collaço

The Vessel — 154
Sharon Soares

Symbiosis — 161
Sheela Jaywant

Cashew Nuts — 172
Joaquim Dias

Not Mum's Jaw — 184
Fatima Noronha

Introduction

"*Quem conta um conto acrescenta um ponto*". Whoever tells a story adds at least a dot to it. This is a Portuguese expression that speaks of the creativity of a narrator, and the impetus that nudges each one of us to add something culled from our own experience to the traditional tales or common events of the day.

The Story accompanies us all through life. As children we are eager to listen to fantastic tales from popular imagination, as adults we are keen to create our own stories rooted in our experience of life, and in old age we yearn to transmit the wisdom of generations.

The Story lives in every literature, since it is, in essence, a form that the most significant world writers cultivate with greater or lesser intensity, but always with great outreach. This is the way it is in Portugal, it is the way it is in India, and also, to some measure or the other, all over the world.

Quite captivated by the genre of the Short Story and aware of the interest this form enjoys among writers in Goa, I was keen to undertake a project that would nurture the creativity of people in Goa in this field and would contribute to deepen a sense of the identity of Goa.

In the planning of the first Fundaçao Oriente Short Story Competition held in Goa in 2011, I was fortunate to count on the support and encouragement of Dr. Maria Aurora Couto. She facilitated, thanks to her profound understanding of Goan society, the process of approaching the right channels so as to turn this into a concrete initiative. It was thanks to her that I received collaboration from the then Editor of O Heraldo, Ashwin Tombat, who was supportive of the launch of a Short Story Competition right from the word go. While promoting this initiative, I was fortunate to have access to the brilliant energy of Savia Viegas: she was instrumental in encouraging and refining the story-telling skills of the participants through a Workshop on Creative Writing.

The Competition galvanized support from a number of institutions. Their representatives formed the jury—Isabel Santa Rita Vas (Fundação Oriente), Vishram Gupte (Herald daily), Damodar Mauzo (Konkani Bhasha Mandal) and José Lourenço (Goa Writers)—shared the enthusiasm of the competitors through their own labour, which was painstaking, serious, and yet enjoyable. These jury members enthusiastically selected the best short stories from among the 67 entries that had been received—in Konkani, Portuguese and English. The multiplicity of languages was based on the very first assumption that Goan culture is multi-lingual.

The discovery of new talent was a great delight. The work of the team was admirable, and the dedication—especially on the part of José Lourenço and Isabel Santa Rita Vás in coordinating the publication of this anthology—is greatly appreciated. This turned out to be one of the most interesting and pleasant projects, among the many that the Delegation of the Fundação Oriente in Goa engages itself with.

We are convinced that the 22 Short Stories that have been edited and published, bring to contemporary Goan literature a touch of freshness and dynamism that will not go unnoticed in days to come. The recognition of new values and the affirmation of yet others, add up to an immense hope.

Last, but certainly not the least, I would like to highlight the collaboration and support lent by Broadway Book Centre and Khalil Ahmed, which made this edition possible. A special word of thanks for Yvonne Rebello of Fundação Oriente whose diligent work helped put together so many voices into print.

I am truly delighted that all the participants in the Short Story Competition 2011 have added, thanks to their tremendous creative energy, new Stories to the Story.

Eduardo Kol de Carvalho
Delegate, Fundação Oriente - Goa
Panjim, November 2013

Introdução

"*Quem conta um conto acrescenta um ponto*". Esta é a máxima portuguesa que exprime a criatividade do narrador e o ímpeto de cada um em adicionar as suas vivências às histórias tradicionais ou acontecimentos comuns.

O Conto acompanha-nos na vida. Em crianças queremos ouvir dos mais velhos as histórias fantásticas do imaginário popular, em adultos não perdemos a oportunidade de criar as nossas próprias histórias baseadas numa experiência de vida e na velhice estamos preparados para transmitir a sabedoria das gerações.

O Conto está presente em todas as literaturas, pois é uma forma essencial dos mais importantes escritores universais que o cultivem com maior ou menor intensidade, mas sempre com grande projecção. É assim em Portugal, é assim na Índia, é assim um pouco por todo o mundo.

Imbuído do gosto pelo Conto e consciente do interesse deste na literatura goesa, empenhei-me em desenvolver um projecto que fomentasse a criatividade dos goeses em torno do conto e contribuísse para o aprofundamento da identidade de Goa.

Na fase decisiva do lançamento do Concurso de Contos contei com o apoio da Dra. Maria Aurora Couto que me incentivou a formalizar o projecto e facilitou, com o seu profundo conhecimento da sociedade goesa, os canais próprios para a concretização da iniciativa. A ela fico a dever a colaboração de Ashwin Tombat então Director de "O Heraldo" que desde a primeira hora apoiou a ideia do lançamento de um Concurso de Contos. A sua saída deste importante diário afectaria a continuidade da colaboração, mas não o sucesso da iniciativa. A promover a iniciativa contei com o brilhantismo de Sávia Viegas que soube incutir nos participantes da Oficina de Escrita Criativa o saber escrever e o saber contar. Depois juntaram-se ao projecto uma maravilhosa equipa que como júri soube com entusiasmo seleccionar as melhores histórias entre os 67 Contos que foram submetidos a concurso, em concani, português ou inglês, porque desde a primeira hora se assumiu que a cultura goesa é multilingue.

Isabel Santa-Rita Vas pela Fundação Oriente, Vishram Gupte pelo Heraldo, Damodar Mauzo pela Konkani Basha Mandal e José Lourenço pelo Goa Writers Group, representando várias organizações porque o Concurso galvanizou o apoio de várias instituições, conseguiram prolongar o entusiasmo dos concorrentes num trabalho escrupuloso, sério, mas também divertido, onde a descoberta de talentos foi uma constante. Quer na fase de selecção quer posteriormente no apoio à concretização da presente Antologia, o seu trabalho foi essencial e a dedicação, sobretudo de José Lourenço e Isabel Santa-Rita Vas inexcedível, tornando este projecto num dos mais interessantes e agradáveis entre os muitos com que a Delegação da Fundação Oriente na Índia se entretém.

Cremos que os 22 contos agora editados trazem à literatura goesa contemporânea uma frescura e um dinamismo que não passará despercebido no futuro. O reconhecimento de novos valores ou a afirmação de outros, é para nós uma imensa esperança.

Por último e não menos importante, não posso deixar de relevar o apoio da Broadway Book Centre e de Khalil Ahmed cuja colaboração tornou possível esta edição, de agradecer à Yvonne Rebello que diligentemente pôs todas as partes em sintonia e naturalmente felicitar todos os participantes do Concurso de Contos 2011, que através da sua criatividade acrescentaram novos Contos aos Contos.

Eduardo Kol de Carvalho
Delegado, Fundação Oriente
Pangim, Novembro de 2013

Mr Secondhand
Manohar Shetty

When Cajetan Xavier sold his ten-year-old Vespa to buy a ten-year-old Maruti 800 it came as no surprise to the other residents of St Jerome's Colony in Dona Paula. The wiry frame of Cajetan put-putting on his ageing scooter up the steep slope before the National Institute of Oceanography and in the hashtag streets of Panjim was a familiar sight. In the colony itself he was a well-known figure as he tinkered with the old scooter, injecting it with a few more months of sustenance in his crowded makeshift garage or as he rode up the slope to his house, the chassis, backseat and handlebars loaded with bags of his weekly provisions. Other residents passing by in their swanky cars would often gesture, asking if he needed any help with his load, but Caji was an independent sort and he would simply wave them on. They were now pleased and relieved to see him in the comparative safety of his car. A secondhand car undoubtedly, but still safer than that old, rundown Vespa.

A sixty-year-old bachelor, Caji loved above all to tinker about in that garage and around his small bungalow that he had bought some twenty years ago from a couple who had migrated to Abu Dhabi. He would be seen constantly in and around the place, applying a coat of paint to the outer walls or hammering away as he repaired some odd bits of old furniture. Twenty years ago Cajetan had taken early retirement as the vice principal of a Portuguese-run school in Beira, Mozambique and returned to his homeland. Unusually for a Goan, he had no immediate relatives in the place of his birth. His forefathers hailed from the village of Chinchinim in Salcete but even there he had only a few distant cousins, second or third removed, with whom he had lost all contact.

Cajetan was quite content to live all alone at St Jerome's with a few daguerreotypes of his ancestors—in tailcoats, hoary moustaches and hats—hanging from the walls of his dining room. He hired no maids and did his own frugal cooking, swept and swabbed his own floors, and kept his garbage out in the green and black dustbins provided by the Panjim municipal corporation. He attended Sunday Mass regularly in the village chapel nearby in his grey suit, off-white shirt, striped tie and slightly cuffed shoes—his apparel never changing in all the years he had attended Mass at the chapel. The other residents of St Jerome's who were not in the least bit surprised when he bought the second-hand car, wondered if he possessed another suit or formal shirt and tie.

Behind his back they often passed catty comments. On his latest acquisition one said:

"May be the government in Lisbon has doubled his pension."

"At last I think he has dipped into his savings ... Such a skinflint," said another.

"Why can't he buy something new for a change? Even on installments ..." said his immediate neighbour, Hector Gonsalves.

That last comment, even given its waspish tone, was most pertinent. Ever since Cajetan had settled in the colony all those years ago, none of the residents could recall him buying anything new. His purchase of the secondhand car post the sale of his secondhand scooter had followed a set pattern. His fellow residents knew that all the furniture in his house had been bought secondhand, some of it from the previous owner of the house and other pieces from households who had migrated to the Middle East or to Canada. Even the fans, the refrigerator, the cooking gas stove and the mixer-juicer had all been bought from previous owners. There were rumours in the colony that even his clothes, including the Sunday suit and shoes, had been bought secondhand from Chor Bazaar in Bombay. No one knew for sure the antecedents of his crockery and cutlery. Some of the residents were even convinced that they had all been bequeathed to him by some kind families in Beira. To be fair to the Jeromites (as they called themselves) they were not off the mark on the used origins of Caji's belongings, and on his cognomen 'Mr Secondhand'.

Cajetan indeed harboured a compulsive fondness for used goods. But it was not a proclivity born out of stinginess or financial necessity. Caji simply liked old things and could not bear to discard used goods. He had a knack with discarded stuff, especially old machinery. With a deft touch of his hands and a reservoir of patience, he could inject new life into a discarded fan or air conditioner or carburetor. Cajetan hated throwing out old things and his makeshift garage and backyard was filled with rusted parts of all kinds of machinery—domestic and vehicular. In fact in Mozambique, he had gained a reputation as something of a miracle worker with obsolete trucks and cars, farm machinery, water pumps and such other mechanical goods. In the school he had taught in, he was well known for fixing old laboratory equipment and machines and the cycles of his many students.

Indeed it was this particular talent for creating born-again machinery that had forced him to flee the country. In the many internecine conflicts that had plagued Mozambique, Caji's services had often been called upon to repair jammed and rusted weaponry and quasi-military vehicles. Caji was a peaceable man, neutral as Bern in his political views, and his services and talent had often been compelled into use by opposing forces. It was this double-edged situation that he found himself in that had finally compelled him to leave Mozambique. He had tried to be impartial in his forced services, but in times of conflict this had proved to be a most inequitable position to be in. Thus he had reluctantly left the country and his chosen vocation. But in return for his many years of service, the Portuguese government still sent him his monthly pension. And he came away to Goa with his knack of repairing old machinery and other goods still intact. When any of the residents of St Jerome approached him with a faulty mixer-cum-grinder or table fan, Caji was always willing to extend a helping hand. And as he never charged for his services, there was an uncharitable and rather mean element to his nickname 'Mr Secondhand'.

Caji now enjoyed the comfort of his old car. With his adroit and versatile hands he had streamlined the engine, fixed the headlights with workable bulbs, set right the brake linings and stitched a tear in the backseat. He had loved his trusted Vespa, but had been forced to get rid of it not because it had turned unreliable and obsolete, but because of a new found status he had recently acquired—or was about to acquire. The clothes he wore, though old and worn, were now always freshly washed and ironed. And his shoes of late had acquired a shiny new look. Not that Caji was sloppy or untidily dressed in the past; it was only now that he took extra care with his demeanour and general appearance. Even the Maruti 800 had acquired a fresh coat of bright yellow paint, cadged no doubt from leftovers from friendly garages and Maruti repair facilities, but still in his capable hands made to extend to the length and breadth of his car. Only a few like the nosey and sharp as a pine-leaf Isobel Cotta noticed the change in Caji's outlook and general behaviour.

"There is something afoot with Caji," she said in a voice as tangy and astringent as cashew fruit. "He actually smiled and wished me good morning."

"Maybe he has received a Christmas bonus in his pension. That's why he could buy that car," said her friend Lavina, a retired clerk from the Cooperative Bank of Mapusa.

"He seems just the same to me," said Winston Dourado who sold life insurance policies. "He still pays his premiums on the dot."

"Something is definitely afoot," repeated Isobel, pursing her lips.

It was two weeks later that the 'something afoot' took a clear and startling direction. The entire colony was agog with a shudder of excitement when each of the residents found an invitation card in their mailboxes. The card, embossed with silver bells at its four corners, simply read:

John and Joanna Pacheco Graciously Invite You
to the Nuptials of Their Daughter
Christobel with Cajetan Xavier
Son of (Late) Martin and
(Late) Belinda Xavier (Chinchinim)
On January 25
At the Church of Mary Immaculate Conception,

Municipal Square, Panjim
At 5.30 pm
Followed by Cocktails and Dinner
at the Taj Holiday Village, Candolim
At 8.30 pm
No Presents Please

Though impressed by the Taj location and the polished tone of the invitation, the very first questions that the stunned residents of St Jerome's asked were, of course: "Who is Christobel Pacheco?" and "How old is she?" They wondered if she was the daughter of the Pachecos of Betalbatim village who owned "Pacheco Wines and Spirits" in the tinto. Or was she from the Pachecos of Rivona who had recently migrated to Portugal? Even with all their networking and crosschecking and church connections the Jeromites could not figure out the provenance of the bride. Till one evening, Isobel and Lavina, armed with flowers and a bottle of wine, knocked on Cajetan's door. He welcomed them warmly and invited them to sit on his carved, refurbished love seat—or that is what Isobel imagined it to be.

After a few congratulatory offerings and some graceless hints, Caji opened up a little. He told them that the Pachecos were old friends and colleagues from Mozambique. And Christobel had been a primary school teacher in the very school he had taught in for many years in Beira. The two ladies told Caji how thrilled they were at this late union of two loving souls, with Lavina interjecting with the rather impolite remark: "Better late than never". In his open happiness, the remark seemed to have no effect on Cajetan who even divulged what they most wanted to hear: "She is 54, six years my junior ..." After the pair left with this precious bit of news, Isobel remarked: "54? Mr Secondhand ties the knot with Miss Secondhand!"

This rather predictable joke spread like a summer land clearing fire among the Jeromites, which was supplemented by: "Better late than never." Another said, "Old wine tastes better." Another wondered rather crudely if "Caji could rise to the occasion", But knowing Caji's frugal disposition, they were all agreed that this would be far from a lavish wedding. In this they were all mistaken.

At the ceremony itself, among the older men, the polite good wishes turned to envy when they saw Christobel. Tall and stately, with dark, luminous hair, she smiled shyly as she accompanied Caji attired in a brand new double-breasted suit, waistcoat and tie and spanking new shoes, walking down the aisle of the church of Our Lady of Immaculate Conception in Panjim. And the reception that followed in the five-star hotel was truly grand with a six-minute-long fireworks display and a sumptuous dinner. And a most energetic and convivial wedding march, with the bride's father giving a touching and humorous toast with remarks on 'fine, mellow old spirit' and 'the wisdom that comes with age'.

The bride herself was most gracious, mingling diffidently with the other guests, speaking to those who knew the language in a Portuguese as refined and eloquent as any spoken by them. A few of course, sat in a corner with their overweight and jaded husbands, remarking on her fair complexion and wondering if she had any Portuguese blood. That this allegation was wholly untrue did not prevent Isobel from making an acid comment on 'oversexed' Portuguese officers stationed in Maputo and Beira.

Such unpleasant remarks and the envy of over-the-hill spouses had no effect on the newly married couple. As soon as they had settled into Caji's bungalow, Christobel set to work. She deweeded the garden, got the interiors of the house repainted, bought some (spanking new) kitchen equipment, imposed some sort of order into the garage-cum-dumpyard and quite easily convinced her husband to make a down payment on a new Maruti car—with a substantial advance from her parents. And though Christobel, without her bridal make-up, looked closer to her age, there was an unbridled energy about her. She chatted with her neighbours and remained on cordial terms with her fellow Jeromites. There were rumours that she had been married before and that her previous husband had disappeared in the numerous civil wars that had besieged Mozambique, reinforcing the joke of Mr Secondhand acquiring a second-hand bride.

But Caji knew better. The Portuguese, despite all their failings, were masters at keeping records. Records of births, deaths and marital status. And Caji still maintained contacts with the church and old friends at the registry in Beira. But in their newfound and profound happiness, the newly married couple didn't give a fig—or a fig-leaf—for unfounded gossip or past history. Indeed they were like nervous but giggly teenagers in their exploration of unknown territory. Their untried concupiscence reached their most tender depths. And Caji being Caji, he often ate the leftovers from Christobel's plate and loved the taste of melted ice-cream on her tongue.

'Mr Secondhand' won the second prize at the Fundação Oriente Short Story Competition 2011.

Mushrooms

Hemant Aiya

It was a hot summer. Onvall had just placed a pot on the fire. Her husband Tamddo, back from the feni still, was lolling around in the front yard. These days he was not beating Onvall, asking for money as usual. Even if he had thrashed her, where did she have any money! In these days of the cashew harvest, alcohol was available in plenty here. Many land owners set up stills for brewing cashew feni. The village drunkards were good for stoking the fire and to tend to the distilling pots in exchange for liquor as wages. The liquor stills run and the drunkards get their fill. The drunkards' wives too are left in peace; they don't get beaten up. Summer would last for just two to three months, but everyone needed them badly. Once the cashew seed prices rose, even the summer heat would be cooler than the heat of money!

But Onvall had no cashew trees. The other day she had gone to steal Sukddo's cashews. Sukddo spotted her. He had a shotgun in his hand. In the low light of dusk, he may not have known whether it was a man or a woman who had entered his cashew grove. He just let loose two rounds of fire in her direction. Onvall shivered, thinking of that incident. If a bullet had to hit her, what would have become of her two sons? This left her shaken up. Just then, her boys came running to her. The younger lad was three-and-a-half years old. He was soaked in sweat. Onvall pulled him close and wiped his perspiring face with the end of her soiled sari.

"Avo! I am hungry!" cried her elder son.

"Me too!" said the younger boy, hugging his mother tightly. The memory of Sukddo firing at her flashed again and she shuddered. She held her sweating son closely and shut her eyes.

Onvall woke up just before dawn. Her younger son had kept crying out of hunger at night. She had alternately slapped him and cajoled him to sleep. Gazing at the innocent sleeping face of her child, something tugged at Onvall's heart. The light of dawn was appearing. She got up. Last evening as she walked home she had looked over Shannu's cashew trees. They were all laden with ripened fruit. An hour-long sortie through the cashew grove would relieve the worries of two or three days. She picked up the rolled towel that served as a pillow at night, tied it around her waist and began walking. She moved quickly, with a pounding heart. The imaginary crack of Sukddo's shotgun echoed in her ears. She paused along the path towards Shannu's cashews, but only for a moment. Then she resumed walking. She stopped at the Mahadev temple on the way and stood for a while with folded hands in front of the deity before continuing. She crossed a small hillock into Shannu's cashew plantation.

"At this time surely no one will come to the cashews," she reassured herself. Yet she looked this way and that, for the morning light would soon brighten. If this work was not done today, the boys would have to sleep hungry again. Thinking of them, she reached out to grasp a branch of a cashew tree and shook it with all her might. The cashew apples began to drop around her. The sound of them falling to the ground gave her some solace. She let go of the branch and began picking the cashews one by one. As she collected them, she plucked their seeds. She loosened the towel from her waist, spread it on the ground and began to place the seeds on it.

From one tree to the next, from there to the third. She plucked six cashew trees and then headed back. Her heart finally stopped pounding. There had been no sign of her husband for the last two days. The boys were still sleeping. She hoisted the bundle of seeds to judge its weight. "This should be about two to three kilos," she thought. She took down a plastic bag that hung from the bamboo rafters of her roof. There was just enough grain to last for the noon's rice gruel. But the morning's work had relieved some of her worry. She lit the kitchen fire. Smoke billowed through the little hut. Both the boys woke up coughing. They rubbed their eyes and looked at their mother.

"Avo, what are you doing?" the elder son asked.

"Aaavo, aavo, I am hungry," the younger boy cried.

"Get up! I'm cooking cunjee for you. Don't you want some? Go to the riverside and do your toilet." These poor lads were starving; there was nothing in their bellies. What would they do going to the river, what toilet would they pass, thought Onvall. Her tears mixed with the tears brought on by the smoke and ran down her cheeks, witnessed only by the kitchen fire.

The season of cashews subsided. The land owners ceased to watch over their trees. Many cashew trees were easily plundered by village boys and wretched people like Onvall. Shaking away at the tree branches easily yielded a kilo of seeds per day. At least two meals of rice gruel could be afforded. The seasonal feni stills too had been dismantled. So Onvall also had to take care of her husband's liquor needs now. These days she gazed worriedly at the sky. Once the rains began, how would she cope with the days of Shravan? She felt anxious, but she would get up every day and go back to the cashew trees she had visited the previous day. The number of seeds collected kept reducing—sometimes she could barely get ten or fifteen. The village shopkeeper too had stopped buying seeds. The kilo of seeds that lay at home had no takers. Still, she would take this lot and try and sell it at the Saturday market. Then she thought, "Let it be. At least during the rains I will be able to roast a few seeds and give them to my sons."

Her elder son came running to her.

"Mother, there's a lot of fish at the panchayat. They are selling it cheap."

She knew they could not afford to buy fish. "Don't we need money to buy fish, son?"

She saw the disappointment in her son's face and said, "Once the rains come, in the Shravan days we may get some money from selling mushrooms."

"Let's not sell the first mushrooms, Avo! Last year you did the same thing. Let us first eat and then sell the rest."

The younger boy who had been listening to his elder brother and his mother speaking also pitched in, "First let us eat, then let us sell!"

He had not yet seen mushrooms, leave alone eat them, but he had often heard his older brother say, "Mother's mushroom bhaji is delicious." Onvall puffed away at the burning twigs in the kitchen. She ignored her sons' eager and hungry looks.

The Jyeshtt and Ashaddh months brought rain. But water only quenched thirst. The month of Shravan was needed to soothe the pangs of hunger. The mushrooms growing on the anthills in the nearby forest had eased hunger for many years in Onvall's house. She walked drenched in the jungle all day, searching the anthills that were familiar to her. But the mushrooms don't just bloom because you wish so, you have to wait patiently. Then perhaps they may grow and if you are blessed, you may get a few to eat. Just because some mushrooms have been spotted they should not be impulsively plucked. A rash move may upset the resident deity of the anthill, a likely snake. All the mushrooms should not be removed, at least one bud must be left behind, or else next year you may not get any, so the elders say.

Trampling twigs and thorny bushes, Onvall searched the spots known to her. It had been raining for a month now, but no anthill had sprouted mushrooms. Even if they had, Onvall had not found any. That evening she returned home completely soaked. Her head ached from roaming all over the forest.

"Avo, did you get any mushrooms?" her elder son asked.

"No, son. I looked all over the forest, but could not find even one," she replied.

"No! You are bluffing, Avo. You must have sold the mushrooms," accused the boy in a tearful voice. He had seen the first mushrooms of the season appear in the market today. Onvall did not reply. She sat down, resting her back against the wooden post at the middle of their hut. Her younger son came and sat on her lap. She blinked playfully at him. Then she closed her eyes and listened to the pitter patter of the rain outside.

A light rain was falling. It was already bright outside. Onvall felt slightly feverish. She picked up her towel and covered her head with it. She made her way to the forest. She walked for quite a while. A few anthills would bloom with mushrooms within the next two days, she reckoned. She went deeper into the woods. Suddenly she saw an anthill that had never flowered before. Today, for the first time in her memory, this anthill was fully covered with mushrooms. Over two hundred umbrella heads, small and large, peered up at Onvall. Her heart filled with joy. She got ready to harvest the earthen mound. As she plucked away, she remembered that it was Saturday, the market day. She left behind a mushroom bud and after bundling her pick into the towel, she ventured even further into the forest. She saw that a couple of anthills had already been harvested by someone else. Solitary mushroom buds on the anthills told her so. Trudging through the entire forest, she plucked another two anthills, which gave her only about forty more stalks. Onvall was happy. She would earn nearly a thousand rupees from this. She snapped off a dozen teak tree leaves and prepared four portions of the mushrooms. Then she walked towards the market.

It was afternoon and still drizzling. She settled down on one side of the bazaar road and spread out her four packets of mushrooms. "I wish I had come a bit earlier," she thought. But she was not disappointed. One who has been fortunate enough to come by mushrooms is never disappointed. Every passerby came to look at her wares. They would ask for the price and haggle over it. They reasoned that many hawkers had come to the market with mushrooms that day. No one was ready to buy a portion for two hundred rupees. They were reluctant to cough up even a hundred rupees for a packet. Onvall began to wonder if her mushrooms would sell at all. Just then a buyer approached her. There was a little boy with her. On seeing the white earth-washed stalks of the mushrooms, the little boy's eyes sparkled. He looked at them with longing.

"How much?" the buyer asked. But her words did not

reach Onvall. She was gazing at the young lad.

"What's the price of these?" the buyer asked again. Again Onvall did not hear her. For a moment she thought the small boy was her younger son. She felt that her son himself was yearning for those mushrooms.

'Hello, can't you hear me? How much?" the customer asked a third time. This time Onvall came to her senses. And blurted out, "Five hundred rupees!"

"Five hundred! So costly!" said the lady and turned away. "Son, we will get cheaper mushrooms further ahead, okay? These ones are not good," she said to her son as she led him away. But the little boy kept looking back at the mushrooms.

"Let's not sell the first mushrooms, Mother! Last year you did the same thing. Let us first eat and then sell the rest!" Still looking at the boy, Onvall recalled her elder son's pleas and her heart was troubled.

"How much?" another buyer stood in front of her.

"Five hundred," replied Onvall, her gaze lingering on the retreating figure of the small boy.

"My God! The seller over there sold for two hundred. Your mushrooms aren't made of gold, are they?"

Onvall was irked. "Buy if you wish. Don't we have mouths to feed? Don't we have children?"

The buyer made a sour face and walked off. Onvall got upset with her own outbursts. "How could I speak like this? What's wrong with me?" she asked herself. But she knew the answer. Somewhere deep inside she felt that these first mushrooms she had found were meant for her children only. But if they ate mushrooms today, where would tomorrow's cunjee come from? This worry loomed large in her mind.

After that, many shoppers came and looked at her mushrooms. A few even bargained. But Onvall did not sell the mushrooms to anyone. She quoted five to six hundred rupees to some of the buyers. Each buyer would remind Onvall of her sons and she would somehow drive them away. But after doing that, she would worry about the next day's needs, decide that the mushrooms *had* to be sold and then await the next buyer. Her heart was in tumult, pulled on one side by her sons' longing and by the impending need for tomorrow's food on the other.

"No, these mushrooms must not be sold. Let tomorrow be. These first mushrooms will be eaten only by my sons. I will cook and serve them for my boys only," she decided. There was no turning back. She would take these packets home. Just then a buyer asked, "Hey, are these mushrooms for sale? I'll take them all for a thousand rupees."

Onvall's heart swelled with happiness. But only for a moment. She had already sworn what to do with the mushrooms. "Sorry, sir," she lied. "They are already sold to someone else, he has gone to get a bag for them." The buyer turned away.

Her decision was firm now. "The mushrooms will be taken home." She wanted to see the eagerness and joy on her children's faces. She rose from her place and began gathering the packets and her towel. Just then an oncoming truck roared towards her. As it gave way to a passing vehicle, the truck veered towards Onvall. She instinctively leapt to one side. But in that instant, the truck tyres ran over her mushrooms. They were completely crushed and lay spattered as though pasted onto the road. Not a single bud could be recovered from the mess. Stunned, Onvall stared at the crushed mushrooms. Her elder son's tearful voice echoed in her head: "No, Avo! You got the mushrooms, but you sold them! You are lying!"

Originally written in Konkani as 'Ollmi'. Translated by José Lourenço .

Angel

Roxanna Pinto

"*Noman Morie kurpen bhorlele, sorvespor tujem thaim asa ...*" To anyone looking through Mr D'Souza's window, the little chocolate-skinned girl saying the Hail Mary would seem to be completely immersed in saying the Rosary. But the truth is, she wasn't.

At seven years, nine months and three days old, Angela was very clear about two things in her life—one, she wanted to be a teacher when she grew up, and two, she wanted to become an angel.

Ai Saiba! Not the curly haired kind with a bow and arrow. That's Cupid, stupid. Big people always seem to get it wrong.

Angela's dream was to become an angel for the Feast of Our Lady of Miracles. Flowing gowns that looked like they were washed in milk, sky-blue sashes, a crown of tiny blossoms on her head, shiny wings ... Angela felt she was born to be an angel; after all, even her name had the word 'Angel' in it.

Angela had known the duties of an angel since she was five. She had practised the walk, the turns, throwing handfuls of scented abolim flowers on the floor, till her mum yelled and made her clean it all up. Years of waiting had finally led to this glorious moment. She had been chosen to be an angel for the feast and it was only three days away.

Angela giggled softly. Mum always heard everything. She shot Angela a dirty look. After the rosary, Angela and her little brother Ronnie queued up to take Mai's, their grandmother's, blessing. Just then the telephone rang shrilly and Mum rushed out of the room to answer it. When she returned, she had a smile on her face. "We have some great news, Angie," shouted Mum (for Mai's benefit). "Your cousin Natasha will be coming down from the US, for the feast."

Angela felt her heart hit the floor. Natasha ('Nuts' as Angela secretly called her) was coming over for the feast. High-heeled, yellow-sunglassed, creamy-skinned, first-in-her-class Natasha was coming over. Snotty little Natasha. Angela took a deep breath. She couldn't handle this alone.

While Mum was busy laying the table for dinner, she slipped across the road to an old crumbling hut. "Lahiraaaa," she hissed. Angela's best friend and fellow troublemaker poked a tentative head through a broken window. "Nuts is coming over again," said Angela plaintively. Lahira squeezed her best friend's hand in sympathy. The last time Nuts had come over, she had managed to upstage Angela's birthday party with her fabulous rendition of Mai's favourite song, 'Claudia'. All the Big People had gushed praises and Mai had given Nuts a gold chain. This time however, Angela would be in the spotlight. She was going to be an angel—for the Feast Mass, no less. With thousands of people watching her. Okay, maybe a hundred. But still, this was Angela's moment in the sun.

Angela woke up the next day to the smell of hot sorpotel and sannas. Tomorrow she would become an angel. God! Why was tomorrow so far away? She heard the sizzle of Mum frying onions for the pulao. Angela's stomach rum-

Angel

bled in anticipation. But then she heard the familiar voice. "Hi there, Anjeee," said Nuts, appearing in the doorway, a vision in purple boots, halter blouse and the trademark yellow sunglasses.

"Natasha," Angela bobbed her head with an air of self-importance. She greeted her cousin with the customary kisses on her cheeks. She then went to the mirror and began brushing her hair. Natasha stared. "Mai told me that you need to brush your hair a hundred times to make it pretty," said Angela, pausing for impact. "I need to look 'gorjus'. I am going to become an angel for the Feast Mass. Thousands of people will be there."

"I remember when I was chosen to sing the national anthem for the mayor of New York," Natasha countered. "He told me that I had the sweetest voice he had everrr heard."

Angela continued brushing her hair silently. She shook off Nuts' comment. Tomorrow she was going to be an angel. Nothing else mattered.

Soon it was lunchtime. Mum sent a pot of steaming hot pulao to Lahira's place. Lahira's father had died four years ago, leaving her mother to provide for three young children. A hot pot of pulao meant a rare feast for the family.

As Angela sat down at the table for lunch, she noticed two things. Mum was smiling a little too much at her and Nuts was nowhere in sight. "Why don't you have the leg?" said Mum, ladling a huge piece of chicken onto her plate. Mum always insisted that the best parts were for the guests. Something was definitely fishy.

"Isn't it great that Natasha's here for the Feast?" asked Mum, casually.

Angela decided that it was best not to answer.

"Your Tia Mildred said that they were very lucky to get

tickets this time. They won't be able to make it again for the next five years," Mum continued.

Inwardly, Angela rejoiced.

"This is Natasha's first Feast. She has never even seen angels. They don't have things like that in the US," said Mum.

Angela waited. Mum was obviously leading up to something.

"Don't you think it would be great if she became an angel for the Feast?" Mum smiled.

This needed a careful answer.

"To be a good angel, you need practice. Besides, the gown won't fit Natasha. She's too tall."

Oops. Not careful enough.

"Oh, I'm not worried about that Angie, you are a fantastic teacher," Mum said quickly. "Remember how you taught Ronnie to sing 'Twinkle twinkle little star'? I'm sure you will train Natasha in no time. Besides, now that you are fine with Natasha becoming an angel, I'll ask Aunty Mafalda to take the hem down. Want some pudding?"

Angela felt her whole world turn upside down. Natasha was smiling at her from near the kitchen. Angela considered her options. Convincing Mum to do anything was impossible. Throwing a tantrum was useless (Mum never paid attention to even three-year-old Ronnie's tantrums). Maybe she could convince Nuts to abandon the idea. This wasn't over yet.

"I'm going to make you an angel for the Feast," Angela told her. "You can have my gown."

Natasha's eyes narrowed. Surely, Anjee wasn't going to give up so easily.

"*Anvaii*, you can't even walk properly!" Angela rolled her eyes dramatically. "I have so much to teach you!"

Hearing all the commotion, Mum quietly popped her head into the bedroom. Angela, Lahira and Natasha were all practising walking with books on their heads, their tiny faces wrinkled in concentration. Makeshift newspaper wings sprouted on their backs. Mum smiled. Her little angel was growing up so fast.

"Now it's time for the dress rehearsal!" proclaimed Angela. Her heart was beating rapidly in anticipation. It was almost 10 o'clock at night—time to get ready for the Feast the next day. The efforts of the entire day hinged on this very moment. Angela carefully handled the gown to Natasha. The girl pulled it over her head and then screamed loudly. She ran around blindly in circles until all the Big People rushed in. Mum helped her out of the gown. A big, confused spider crawled down Natasha's back.

"I h-h-hate s-p-p-p-iders ..." spluttered Natasha. "I'm n-not wearing that gown. I'm n-n-not going to the Feast. I d-don't want to become an angel."

In the corner, Angela bit back a smile. It had been a brilliant idea to put a spider into the gown. That way, she was in the clear. Mum wouldn't suspect a thing. Lahira put her arm around the shivering, sobbing girl. Her voice was soft and soothing, but her accusing eyes darted at Angela.

For the first time, Angela felt a little prick. How did Lahira know? This was her secret.

Fifteen minutes later, Natasha had cried herself to sleep. "Angie, come in here," Mum called out. Angela slowly made her way to the living room. Did Mum know? She waited for the scolding, but Mum said, "Looks like Natasha is terrified of the whole spider episode." Natasha thought her mother looked a little sad. "She will not be able to become an angel. I have spoken to Tia Mafalda and she has altered the gown. You will be the angel tomorrow."

Angela paused, waiting for the news to sink in, for the happy feelings and the rush of excitement to grip her like it did yesterday. But instead she felt empty. Something didn't feel right.

She tossed and turned in her bed the entire night. Angela couldn't forget how bitterly Nuts was crying after the whole episode. If you really thought about it, except for those ugly sunglasses, the girl wasn't *that* bad. Natasha had taught Angela how to fish the last time she had come over. And she had gifted Angela the pink princess dress she had liked from that big shop (the dress with a matching tiara and wand). Angela wondered if she should tell her mother the truth. Mum would tell her to say sorry to her cousin. And she would have to see that smirk on Natasha's face!

Angela was going to become an angel for the Feast mass. But she had never felt less angelic. Angela felt something underneath her pillow. It was a medal of St. Michael, the Archangel. Suddenly it came to her. She knew what she had to do.

The Feast of Our Lady of Miracles, or Milagres as they say in Konkani, is celebrated in Mapusa on the Monday after the second Sunday of Easter. The devotees believe that *Saibinn Māi* performs great miracles. People from all communities travel to the church to pay their respects. Hindus offer oil and garlands, and Catholics say a little prayer at the shrine. On the Feast day, the church square is abuzz with energy and excitement. At the close of the mass, seven children dressed as angels—one leading with a banner and the rest following in line—sprinkle scented flowers (shenvtim, mogrim and abolim), as they lead the priests for the procession.

The priest said the final prayers. It was time for the procession of the angels. Cameras flashed as eager parents jostled to capture these priceless memories.

Angel

Mrs Philo Gomes, the coordinator for the angels, carefully watched the children walk up in pairs. Bruno, holding the banner, Maria and Savio, Francis and Trina, Russell and Angela.

But wait a minute! The girl walking alongside Russell was not Angela. That girl ... she was Dency's neighbour. What was her name? Sweet child ... Lahira.

Angela looked at her Mum and smiled. Mum's eyes seemed to be watering. Angela had quietly slipped out during the costume change and cajoled her kind-hearted best friend to become the angel. She had deserved it.

Angela felt a hand close in warmly on hers. It was Natasha's. It's a wonderful thing about children, their little hearts are too big for grudges. There's no sense of ego, no lingering wounded pride. Sorrys are earnestly meant, easily said, hurts are easily forgiven, forgotten.

As she watched her best friend walk down the aisle, her face bursting into a thousand smiles, Angela truly felt like an angel.

The Dead Donkey
Pralay Bakshi

It was Raju, the pav bhaji vendor, who first spotted the dead donkey under the bridge. It was nearing half past nine, and the city was just about beginning to wake up. Though he normally started business in the evening, he had come that day to reason with Bhau, the local havaldar, who had been insisting on a higher 'cut'. He knew he would eventually have to cough up the money, but was hoping he could postpone it till the season began in November.

At first, he did not quite comprehend the gravity of the dead donkey situation, and felt no more than casual curiosity, as he was to meet Bhau in a few minutes near the bus stop. But as realisation suddenly dawned on him, he experienced a surge of panic.

"If this donkey is not gone by this evening, how will I sell anything?" he thought. "No one will eat from a pav bhaji stall a few steps away from a dead donkey! And not just today; once people come to know, my business will not recover for months! Hai Ram!"

He had to do something, but what? Maybe Bhau could

help. After all, their give-and-take relationship was almost six years old, Bhau was almost a friend. Raju hurried on to the bus stop.

"How are you?" asked Bhau with a grin, when he saw Raju approaching, at a somewhat faster pace than usual.

"There's a problem," said Raju. "There's a dead donkey near my spot!"

"What are you saying, yaar? Chalo, let's take a look!"

The donkey was lying in a small puddle of water, but its body was almost dry. "It must have been taking shelter from the rain last night," deduced Bhau, "that's why it's at this spot. But where did it come from and whose donkey is it?" This was the first chance at doing some detective work that he had got since the night Mrs Gomes' cat ran away, and he was not going to waste it.

"Baba, let all that be, we need to get this away from here!" said Raju, with urgency.

A passer-by on a motorcycle stopped out of curiosity. "Hey, what's this? A dead donkey? Did you kill it?" he asked Raju. Maybe the presence of a havaldar led him to believe that.

"No, no!" protested Raju. "I just found it here, ten minutes ago!"

"Chalo, chalo, keep moving, you'll block the traffic," said Bhau, in an officious tone.

"What traffic?"

"Arre, you're arguing with a policewala, huh? Chalo!"

The motorcyclist sped off, only to stop some distance away. He pulled out his cellphone and made a few calls.

"We'll just call the municipality guys, they'll come and take this away," said Bhau. "I'll call them at about eleven, when they get in to work."

A few more people had gathered and had started pointing at the carcass. "This can't be good," thought Raju.

"Can't we do something sooner? My business will be ruined!" he pleaded.

"I can try, but it will cost some money, boss," said Bhau, sensing an opportunity to make a quick buck. He did know one of the garbage disposal guys at the municipal office, who would probably charge him a hundred rupees. "It'll cost you five hundred," he said.

With a mix of some pleading, negotiating and appealing to their quasi-friendship, Raju managed to bring the amount down to two hundred and fifty rupees. Almost half of the evening's profit, but worth it. Bhau made a quick call. Help was on its way.

"Fifteen minutes," said Bhau. The machinery worked much faster with a little bit of greasing.

The crowd had now grown to about thirty people. A twenty-something man in scruffy jeans and a faded T-shirt pushed forward. He pulled out a camera from a bag and started taking pictures.

"Arre, what are you doing?" threatened Bhau.

The man pulled out an identity card and thrust it in Bhau's face. He was a reporter with a local newspaper. Bhau retreated. Tiny beads of sweat began forming on his forehead. He wished it would start raining.

The reporter continued taking pictures. "This'll probably make it to page six," he thought. Not much happened in the city on a normal day. "Bloody hell, is this what I did my MA in Literature for?" he lamented silently to himself. Still, he was thankful to his friend who had called him earlier with the news. At least he had got here before the others. He tried to think of headline options for the story. The Don(key) is Dead ... Whose Ass is It? ... Please Bray for Him

... How he wished he could stick in such headlines some day. He knew he'd have to go with something quite banal like 'P'City Morning Traffic Disrupted by Dead Donkey'. Oh well.

The garbage truck arrived. Two men in vests stepped out with a large sack. Actually, a man and a boy. They laid the sack down next to the carcass and, lifting it by its legs, transferred it on to the sack. They then moved the sack from under the bridge to the middle of the street, next to the truck.

'*Chamiya, naach naach naach ...*' the latest chartbuster burst out loudly. The man reached into his pocket and pulled out a cellphone.

"Hello ... haan, sir ... yes, sir ... we are at the site, sir ... ah, ok... so, what to do sir?... ah, no problem, sir... ok, sir." The man signalled to the boy. The two took the carcass off the sack and placed it back on the street. Folded sack secured, the two headed back to the truck.

Raju rushed towards them. Bhau followed.

"Arre, arre, take this thing with you!" pleaded Raju.

"Sorry, can't do. Boss's orders," said the man.

"What's the problem?" asked Bhau.

"My boss got a call from the neighbouring town's panchayat. It seems we can't take this to their dumping ground anymore. My friend just got beaten up last week."

The garbage wars had been going on for a while. Nobody wanted the stink in their backyard, it seems. What it really meant was that until the right amount of money exchanged hands, this was going to be a touchy subject.

As the hours passed, the news spread across the city. It was a small place, everybody knew everybody. Three local television crews arrived, set up and started doing live updates. The local councillor, who had arrived minutes ago, was irate when he heard of the non-cooperation by the neighbouring panchayat.

"We had an agreement!" he bellowed into the cameras, "How can they suddenly stop us just because the deadline has passed? These things take time to sort out! They should understand! For all I know, the donkey probably strayed in from their area! It's a village area after all! We don't have donkeys in the city!"

Camera crews reached the office of the panchayat too. "These are baseless accusations," an official said. "Nobody has reported a missing donkey in our town! If he says this is our donkey, let him prove it!"

Behind closed doors, more powerful men began putting their minds to the situation. The story crept on to the national news channels. The party high commands of both the ruling and opposition parties called up their local leaders. The opposition was trying to figure out what strategy would help them get maximum mileage out of the situation. Somebody suggested a bandh. "We must refuse to be treated like donkeys anymore," said a senior leader. "This is a chance for us to topple the government." In the ruling party office, whispers of another coup were doing the rounds: "He has lost control of the situation. We need a better leader."

A third party, of self-proclaimed sons of the soil, had a brainwave. "This is clearly an immigrant issue," declared their spokesperson. "All dhobis in the city are from the northern states, and these washermen are the ones that use donkeys to carry around clothes. They have clearly overburdened a native donkey. We will simply not stand for it! Or, worse still, they have brought the donkey from outside the state. This is a serious menace. How long must we support donkeys from other states? We don't want them doing the jobs that our donkeys should be doing!" Almost inevitably, a couple of animal rights groups jumped in. There was enough meat in the story to investigate animal cruelty, negligence, the ethical issues around the use of donkeys and the need for offering them shelter. "Let's demand a complete ban on the use of donkeys across the country. Just because they have been carrying clothes, firewood and pilgrims for centuries does not mean that they should continue to do so. It is time we fought for their rights!"

The story spread like wildfire over the Internet. Fan pages, blogs and obituary pages rose up all over the country. Somebody important threatened to go on an indefinite fast, no one was quite sure why and no one really bothered to clarify. It was only a matter of time before someone did a Google search using the words 'donkeys' and 'endangered' to come up with a list of names of endangered donkey types: Poitou, Martina Franca, African Ass ... And as often happens with Internet Chinese whispers, an innocent question on some blog asking if the dead donkey might be from an endangered species quickly turned into a raging conviction that it was. In fact, a sub-species name and the fact that there were only one thousand four hundred and eleven of these donkeys left in the country soon started doing the rounds. In came the environmentalists and animal conservationists.

A mere ten hours had passed since Raju had first come across the donkey. He was now actually quite pleased. As the man who had come across the donkey first, his face had been plastered across all the TV channels since that morning. Business would be fantastic—he could probably rent a shop soon, or at least move to another location immediately. He was now a celebrity pav bhaji vendor.

The donkey lay in the middle of the street, where the garbage disposal men had dragged it. As the light faded, a few drops of rain began to fall. The crowd began dispersing, looking for shelter. People who did not have umbrellas crowded under the bridge. The rain started to get heavier.

It was dark and the rain made visibility poorer. Nobody really noticed that the donkey had begun to stir. Slowly, rising from its stupor, it groggily got up and unsteadily walked away. The few who noticed probably did not realise it at that time—they may have thought that it was a vehicle or maybe some other animal. By the time the rain stopped, the donkey was gone.

It was a mystery. No one quite knew what had happened, how a dead donkey had simply gotten up and left. After about four days, the brouhaha eventually died down—the TV channels found another miracle to cover, the politicians moved on to the language debate and the newspapers found a local harvest festival more than enough to fill their pages.

Meanwhile, about five kilometres from the bridge where the 'dead' donkey was found, a young man in a lab coat heaved a sigh of relief. Five days ago, in his hurry to meet his girlfriend after work, he had left the door to the store room ajar. Luckily, when he returned the next morning, nothing had gone missing. Well, almost nothing.

Except for two packs of sleeping pills. But then, who would miss something like that at such a large pharmaceutical factory?

Pause

Nayana Adarkar

"Shradha, Sir has asked you to complete this file today at any cost," said Devidas, slamming the file on her table. Shradha picked up the file and looked at it. "Didn't Sir give this file to you to complete? You haven't even touched it," she said, irritated.

"Today he has asked you to do it, right? So you do it!" said Devidas indifferently.

"He had asked you first. Couldn't you do it?" Shradha persisted.

"Just do what you have been told. Don't give me any talk."

Devidas' words infuriated Shradha. What did he think of himself? He could not even respect her age. She thought of getting up and returning the file to the boss. Suddenly Devidas picked up the file and turned towards their supervisor's cabin.

"That's it! He's gone to tell tales to the boss. They get along well and make me the scapegoat. Rogues!" Shradha fretted. And that's how it turned out. Shradha was called to the cabin.

"Haven't you been told to complete this file today?" Her boss peered at her through his glasses.

"Sir, you had given this file to Devidas yesterday. But he hasn't even touched it." Despite knowing that it would not help much, Shradha voiced her complaint.

"I don't want to hear all that. Keep in mind that this is company work and you are a company employee. I don't want any excuses." As the boss scolded her, a smirk spread on Devidas' face. Seeing that look, Shradha flushed with rage. "So when you gave this work to Devidas it wasn't company work then?"

"Look here. Don't give me that street talk. I'll tell you one thing. He is your senior. You have to obey him." The boss' orders inflamed Shradha. She felt like retorting with a barrage of words but said nothing. Only her lips quivered, as did her body.

She returned to her cabin. "Rascal! He wears his badge of seniority and dumps all the work on me." Her head felt heavy and hot. Her heart started pounding. She felt hot flushes spreading all over her lips and ears.

"Damn it, this sickness is back again." She sat down, gripping the table with both hands. This was happening very often of late. "They are symptoms of menopause," Dr Brenda had told her, and had also prescribed some medicines.

Menopause—Dr Brenda had explained—"Men O Pause. Stop now, you men. This woman's body is no longer young." Dr Brenda had laughed heartily as she said this. But Shradha's heart had filled with fear then. The images of many old women flashed before her eyes. Those memories disturbed her now. Old age had begun. After its purpose is over, does the body grow old? And the mind? Wasn't there any link between the body and mind? In her wandering thoughts she did not hear what Devidas was saying.

"Sit there thinking and wasting time and then complain that it's getting late. After you have finished the file, keep it in this drawer," he said, pointing to his table. "As you grow older, your memory also scatters, and this mess gets worse every day."

Shradha felt like slapping him. But she restrained herself. She was wounded though. Whom could she speak to? Her boss? He was always sharpening cruel words to fling at whoever was available. Devidas was just waiting for such chances. "Brute! Does not even know how to respect age. Just taunts and offends with every word."

Suddenly she recalled what her boss had said. "Don't give me that street talk." She glanced at Devidas. He was flirting with someone over the phone. "Street talk!" Shradha mumbled through clenched teeth.

For many years she had quietly borne the drudgery handed out to her by these two men. She had suffered all the work they dumped on her on the pretext of their seniority. She had shrugged off and tolerated all that. But of late she couldn't bear it. She would get angry quickly and respond to provocation with fiery words. Everyone would then call her quarrelsome. And sometimes, even for a small reason, she would break down in tears, her mind filled with despair. There wasn't even a chance of telling all this to Vinod. He simply didn't have time. Other than his office and the club, nothing else mattered to him. Only when their daughter returned home from her hostel would he cease his visits to the club. If she complained to him he would probably say, "You have indeed grown old. Why should you get so angry if he said these things? If you feel upset, take voluntary retirement. And stay at home."

There were many other women in the office. A couple of them were about Shradha's age. But they had never experienced this. So this wasn't some kind of illness, was it? Perhaps Dr Brenda wasn't telling her everything. Or perhaps she hadn't diagnosed her properly? Crabs of doubt dug away at the sands of her mind. The air conditioning felt chilly. The AC control was in Devidas' hands. "Could you please switch off the AC?" she requested him.

"Madam, this AC is not installed for you. It is there to cool the computer servers, got it?"

She clenched her teeth. "I know it is for the servers. If you even sneeze slightly, you switch it off!" She lashed back defiantly but, despite herself, tears welled up in her eyes. Shradha was irritated with her own weakness.

She struggled on and somehow finished working on the file. At the end of her office hours she trudged towards the bus stand. She felt very tired. It was unlikely that she would get to rest at home. Vinod must have brought fish to be cooked, as usual. The bus arrived and she got in.

The bus rolled on. Shradha sat with her eyes closed. Behind her closed eyes, her thoughts persisted in grinding away. "It isn't good to get so emotional," Ramita from the Accounts section had scolded her some days back. "Getting angry in a flash, and then weeping in the next moment, what is this!" Even Vinod would say "As you grow older are your nerves also getting tattered?"

Dr Brenda's words began spinning in her head. "Menopause has arrived. Menopause." Ramita too had said, "Damn it. Earlier we had that monthly headache. Now that problem will certainly go away, but now the knees get stiff, the back gets stuck. It's like your whole life hits a pause." "You are growing old," Vidya had said, "That's what menopause is telling you." Sudha appeared before her eyes, "You know, these nights I dream that I am walking around naked. But not a single man even looks at my body." All the other women had laughed at this. You are an old woman, they had mocked her. Vidya had said "Hey, why will they look at your body? It has become like a parched and fallow field." Shradha pictured her own body. Slouched and slovenly. Of late, her waist had expanded quite a bit. Layers of fat padded her buttocks. Her breasts had sagged. Vinod would joke about it at night, "Your body has aged. Like a loosened buckle ..."

As her thoughts meandered, the bus reached the last stop. Weary and depleted, she walked home. She felt like a mango crushed in a pickling jar, all wrinkled and squeezed out.

Vinod was at the door. He was all set to go to the club. On seeing Shradha, he said, "I have brought some good mackerel. Prepare udidmethi."

She felt like throwing herself on her bed, but ...

"Yes, I will do it," she said lifelessly.

"Why are you talking in such a dead way?" Vinod asked her.

"I am not feeling well," she said.

"That's your usual complaint. Throw those mackerel out!" He kick-started the scooter and rode off. He would be back only at ten o'clock. Today he should have stayed home—for her sake. He should have cuddled and held her. Then she would have laid her head on his shoulder and lightened up. But perhaps he wasn't bothered. She remembered her daughter. If she had been here maybe she would have understood. Only a woman can sense another's pain. But she was in her hostel in Pune. And even if she was home, would she really have understood? Or like her husband, would she mock her saying "You've grown old, Ma!"

To avoid any hassles with Vinod, despite her exhaustion, Shradha cooked the mackerel udidmethi. Vinod savoured the dish at dinner. But he did not enquire even once about how she was feeling. Instead he rattled on about the happenings at the club. Shradha had no patience to listen to those stories. But how could she say so? Putting on a mask of interest, she listened to all his talk.

Vinod went to bed. She tidied up the kitchen. When she went to the bedroom and slumped on the bed, Vinod tried to pull her closer, but she turned away. He grumbled, "It wasn't for no reason that kings in those days had two wives ..." and soon fell asleep. But his words reminded Shradha of her impending old age. Dr Brenda's words flashed again ...

"It's menopause ... menopause."

"This is the first stage of old age."

"We have grown old, dear."

"Menopause means a pause in life."

"My dear, the youth of our bodies is gone, from now on it's only a dry hard road."

All these words began spinning in her mind. "Old ... old ..." A volley of these words set her heart afire. She felt the heat. Her heart began to pound. Waves of heat flushed across her face and ears. Terrified, she flung her arm around Vinod. He pushed her away with a snort and resumed snoring. That broke Shradha's heart. Her wounded soul poured out in tears for a long while. Sometime before dawn she fell asleep.

She dreamt.

She, Sudha, Ramita and Vidya are walking in a vast meadow, stark naked. Dr Brenda is standing with her stethoscope around her neck and a stick in hand. Many people are standing around. Dr Brenda is whispering to those bystanders, "They have gone into menopause ... menopause ..." People are pointing fingers at them and murmuring. Their muttering rises to a shrill chant ... "Old age ... old age ..." The women are all frightened. Suddenly Shradha runs to Dr Brenda, grabs her stick and begins to scratch out some words on the ground, "*Me no pause*. I will not stop ..." She waves the stick in her hand and shouts at the bystanders, "I will not stop. My body may have completed its duty. It has paused. But my mind? My mind has kept all my dreams and desires suppressed for so long. That mind is free now. Free from the duties of the body and the demands of the world. I now want to reclaim my life. I want to fearlessly paint my free thoughts on the canvas of the sky." She holds the stick high and proclaims, "Me no pause ... Me no pause ... Me no pause."

She approaches Ramita, Vidya and Sudha. The three women look at her with awe. "Come on, let us leap into the sky together!" As she beckons, they all come closer. Holding each other's hands, they leap into the sky and begin to fly like birds. The people who had been murmuring at them all this while begin to applaud cheerily.

As dawn began painting the sky with free colours, a broad smile of happiness spread on Shradha's half-asleep face.

Originally written in Konkani as 'Pause'. Translated by José Lourenço.

Son of the Soil
Nikhil Ribeiro

Ricardo shifted uneasily on the old wooden bench in the balcão of his house. He could feel a few jagged splinters of the wood through his pants. Everyone else in his village had replaced their old benches with shiny, easy-to-clean ones of polished cement. Only his father remained stubbornly entrenched in the old ways.

It was early evening and his father was sitting outside too. His back was ramrod straight and although he was facing the road, his eyes were not focused on the people who occasionally passed by. "Very likely he is sitting there because three generations of Nazareth men before him did the same. What an old fool. Those men sat there to accept offerings from their gaunkars, to settle disputes or to have a drink with friends. But he sits alone, a slave to tradition," thought Ricardo as he turned onto his stomach to look at his father.

"Hey, Pa!" he called out. The old man's back got a little straighter as his eyes shifted to his sprawling son. "No doubt he is more interested right now in what people on the road will think of me than in what I have to say," thought Ricardo.

"When are you going to get these benches fixed?" asked Ricardo.

"Fixed? They don't look broken to me."

"Come on, Pa. You know what I mean. These benches are so poky and uncomfortable to sleep on. Every rainy season they become soggy and mouldy."

"They are not meant for sleeping on. Besides they were good enough for three generations of Nazareths and they are good enough for me. If *you* want to fix them then get a job, earn some money and get it done yourself."

Ricardo swatted angrily at a mosquito and picked its crushed remains off his arm. The old man invariably brought around every conversation to Ricardo's unemployment.

"If you had given the money for my seat at Garden City College instead of Xavier's, I would have got a job easily even before I passed out. But you didn't pay and so I had to look for a job in Bombay. I tried very hard," said Ricardo.

"How many times to tell you?' said his father. "We didn't have the money to pay those greedy robbers. And why Bombay? There is plenty of work here itself for which you don't need college."

"Oh, so should I go and tell Gopu to stop digging ditches and painting walls so that I can do it? *Huh?*"

"People respect Gopu more than you. Do you know how many people ask me about you? They want to know if you have settled down. How can I tell them that you don't even have a job?"

"Tell them that you spoiled my future by not paying the college capitation fee. As if five lakhs is so much. What a miser you are," answered Ricardo.

Even as he finished speaking, he realised that he had gone too far. "Enough!" roared his father and made as if to slap him. His grey hair, remarkably intact for a man of his age, fell about his face in disarray. Ricardo merely laughed. There was a time when he would have flinched and his father would have retreated in merciful magnanimity. But it was years since the old man had struck fear in his son's heart.

The old man stood over his son with an expression of rage spread across his wrinkly plumpness. Ricardo noticed that his mother had appeared on the scene and was standing behind his father. She stood there uncertainly and after a few seconds finally, mercifully, said, "Come on Socorro. Don't get excited. It's not good for your age." Socorro turned without a word and headed indoors.

His mother gazed at her husband's receding bulk and said, "Why you always bring that up? You know how angry he gets."

Ricardo shrugged and said, "He deserved it. Always insulting me."

She sighed deeply and followed her husband indoors.

He had not meant to anger the old man today. In fact, he was trying to maintain a cordial relationship with him. He had asked his father for some money a few months back. He had solemnly taken his father into the hall and closed the door on his inquisitive mother saying, "Ma, it's about some business thing. You will not understand and then simply get worried." His father had allowed himself to be led into the hall and seated. Ricardo began to lay out his plans nervously. His voice occasionally shook and he hoped that his father would not notice and if he did, that he would mistake it for passion. He spoke at great length and tried to instil some of the excitement he felt into his father. His father had listened and nodded, but Ricardo had barely finished speaking when he said, "No, I have better use for my money."

Ricardo was furious—the way the old man had allowed himself to be serenaded! As if it was all a joke to him. He rushed out of the hall, brushing aside his mother's queries ("What happened, baba? What Papa said?") and locked himself in his room.

After two days of curtly telling his mother to leave him alone, he realised that he could use her help.

"Okay, I will speak to him, but you also please behave properly. Don't irritate him unnecessarily," she had said and laughed when he hugged her spontaneously.

In the confines of his hug she dropped her voice to a whisper and said, "Ricardo baba, this restaurant business is safe, no?"

"Of course, Ma!" he had responded irritably and then picked up a magazine to indicate he was done with her.

As the days passed, however, his mother seemed to be making very little progress with Socorro. Instead, she began to cook increasingly exotic (to their household) dishes like vindaloo and sorpotel and offered tit-bits of culinary wisdom at the dinner table that made him cringe with embarrassment:

"While preparing xacuti, it's better to buy the freshly prepared masala from Mapusa rather than the readymade stuff—makes a huge difference."

"Don't use too much vinegar in the sorpotel unless you want to make people sick."

She even brought him the cookbooks that she normally kept wrapped in old paper and hidden away in cupboards. He left them untouched where she had kept them on his bed. After a week he kicked them onto the floor.

Now, left alone in the balcão, Ricardo looked around lazily to see if anybody was passing by on the road and then touched himself, thinking, "Once Papa gives me the money, I can finally get my restaurant business started with Joao. Then when the restaurant is running nicely I can start a cyber-cafe. That will be my own business—better have something that I alone have absolute control of. Right now only Sangodkar Infocom is there and they don't even have flat-screens and laser mice. I will keep the latest—"

"Patrão," said somebody in a husky non-Goan accent. Ricardo started and pulled his hand away quickly. He had got carried away. "Luckily it's only Gopu," he thought with relief. He looked carefully at Gopu to see if he had noticed anything, but his face was a rugged mask of sweat and dirt.

"*Kitem re? Kitem zai?*" asked Ricardo irritably.

"*Bai asa?*" asked Gopu politely.

Idiot probably wants to get paid before he goes to his village, thought Ricardo.

"*Hangach rav,*" he said and went indoors to fetch his mother.

The door to his parents' bedroom was closed. Locked doors were unusual in their household and so Ricardo hesitated before knocking. He heard his mother speaking and thought, "She is talking to him now. She must be convincing that old miser at this very moment." He leaned in close toward the door and tried to hear the conversation.

Bombay had been a terrible experience. Ricardo had overstayed his welcome in David's flat.

The fool should have been clear about what he meant by "Come stay with me as long as you like." Three weeks in a one bedroom flat with two other guys, water for two hours a day (4am to 6am) and no fan was not enough torture to make

Ricardo go back to his father with his tail between his legs. He planned to stick it out and stay with David for as long as it took to find a job in Bombay.

Then one day he had woken up at two in the morning and heard his name being spoken softly. Instinctively he remained still and strained to listen to the conversation.

"...*abe yaar*, he is from my village," that was definitely David speaking. "I can't say no to him. You know how these villagers are. Next his mother will ignore my mother at Mass and by evening the whole village will be talking about the latest fight between the bhatkars."

Another voice, probably Bhimsen's, "I know yaar, but there is so little water and that fatty gets up before anyone else and washes his bum nicely. He doesn't even go to office but acts like a big man—waking up early and shaving with his fancy blade."

They laughed softly and then began to talk of something else. Ricardo struggled to control his heaving shoulders and thanked God that he was curled up with his back to them. The next day he lay in bed until the others had woken up and finished getting ready for work.

When David was leaving the flat, Ricardo said, "I will be going back to Goa today, *re*. Am going by the morning bus, will reach Goa late in the evening. Thanks a lot for letting me stay here."

"It will be damn hot ya. Wait until evening and take the night bus, I will reach you to the bus stop after I finish work," David said.

But Ricardo insisted, saying, "My father called me very fast, re. Some property matter. I think he wants my signature."

He left Bombay without shaving or bathing.

On the long ride home in the sweltering hot bus Ricardo

decided that Bombay was not for him. He had grown up hearing tales of self made men like Cosme Matias Menezes who built empires out of nothing. He felt that he too could one day build an empire. "Better to fail at a business rather than work for decades as a escrivão like Papa did, for a salary that even a rickshaw driver would laugh at," he had told his mother.

For no reason other than that he liked food and had eaten at a few good restaurants in Bombay, Ricardo decided to start a restaurant in his village. The idea seized his imagination like nothing ever had before. Plans for it consumed his energy so completely that he did not have time to contemplate the fact that a village the size of his could barely support a grocery store, leave alone a restaurant. All day long he meditated upon things like whether he should serve Chinese food ("Can't imagine big shots like Dr Filipe eating in a cheap Chinese restaurant, better to keep it classy") and whether it would be wise to hire local boys as waiters ("They might resent us if we hire only outsiders but we grew up together and it may be difficult to keep them disciplined and respectful").

He even found a partner, Joao, who was popular, athletic, two years older than Ricardo and had every girl in the village after him. They had become friends during Catechism classes when Joao would copy from him during the tests.

Now all he needed was the money. Joao had said that two lakhs would be enough to start with.

"... It is our last field, Inês," his father's voice was muffled by the ancient wooden door. "If we sell it then we won't be bhatkars anymore."

"I know, Socorro, but Ricardo seems happy and confident about his restaurant idea. You know how depressed he has been since he came back from Bombay after looking so much for a job."

"Ya ya, I know. He wasted so much money going to and fro and walking up and down but had nothing to show for it. So many times I offered to speak to my friends in the Communidade and get him a escrivão's job, but he always refused."

"You know he is not the kind of boy who will like office work. From small he always seemed to be interested in business."

"But why should I sponsor him? We sacrificed so much for him. You know how everyone was telling us not to sell that cashew plantation in Divar. The property's value will double in two years, they said. But I sold it to pay for his college fees and now that ungrateful rascal wants to bleed me dry."

"He does not know about that plantation, Suco," said his mother.

It was true. Ricardo was surprised to hear about it. There was such a dramatic difference in the fees of Garden City College and Xavier's that he assumed his father could easily afford to pay for the latter. "But that's the past," he thought angrily. "That miser is making any excuse not to give me the money."

He was about to leave in despair when his mother began to speak. "Suco, I didn't want to tell you this before, because it will simply raise your blood pressure. But yesterday at the Chapel while the men were chatting, I heard them talking about us. They were saying that the Nazareth family has fallen so low that our son is a bum and that we are too poor to secure his future."

Ricardo marvelled at his mother's cunning. After thirty years of marriage she had learned which buttons to push to get what she wanted.

His father was quiet for a while and then began to speak. "I have tried to be a good man, Inês. I never had much in life. It's true that my ancestors were big bhatkars, but that was hundreds of years ago. Everyone expected me to be a big man—a doctor or an advocate. As if I had all my ancestors' fields and plantations in my back pocket. But I inherited peanuts. The great Nazareths were destroyed by that phenomenon that perpetually plagues the landed gentry—a surfeit of sons. Seven sons in three generations! Good old Ricardo Nazareth's properties were divided and divided and divided until here I am—Socorro Lawrence Nascimento Nazareth—a damned escrivão at the Divar Communidade with one dirty field left!"

His father's voice had risen to a crescendo as he spoke and now he paused for breath. His mother was quiet. Half the words must have gone over Mama's head, thought Ricardo.

"I will be damned if my son is going to be another escrivão too," continued his father, "I am going to sell that field and even dip into our savings if we have to but I will see that my son has the chance that I never did. Then let me see who dares spit on our name!"

Ricardo reeled back from the door. He could scarcely believe it! The old man had finally come through. "He has finally given me my birthright. Joao will be so excited," he thought and rushed past a gaping Gopu and walked rapidly towards the Chapel where he knew he would find Joao.

He could see Joao sitting on the cement benches around the Chapel ground. He was in a group of around six people. The boys were all wearing jerseys and sports shorts. It looked as if they had just finished the evening badminton game and were chatting with some girls from the village.

Ricardo felt a bit nervous seeing the slim and fair girls, but told himself, "I have a reason to be here. I am going to talk to Joao, the most popular guy in the group."

As he approached them Joao noticed him and called out, "Bhatkar! What brings you here?"

"Can I talk to you, re?" asked Ricardo.

"Arrey, don't be shy. Come and tell me," said Joao.

"He's scared of you. Why do you always look so cute?" Joao asked Clarissa playfully. She was a beautiful girl who was wearing skinny jeans and a T-shirt that showed just a hint of stomach skin.

Clarissa blushed and said, "Shut up, pig!" and resumed her conversation with the others. Ricardo lived just three houses away from her but they never spoke to each other, he was too shy to look her in the eye.

"I got that money for the restaurant. That miserly old man finally decided to sell one of our properties and give me the cash we need," said Ricardo. He felt bad to speak of his father like that but Joao often spoke of his father in the same way too.

"*Avoiss!* That's great news!" shouted Joao and put his arm around Ricardo's shoulders.

"We're going to start a business, guys. Meet my new partner," he announced to the group.

"What kind of business?" asked Clarissa, her eyes on Ricardo.

"A restaurant," answered Ricardo.

" ... and bar," added Joao.

Ricardo was unsettled. His father was a teetotaller and might not look kindly on the restaurant having a bar. Eventually most of the group left and only Ricardo, Joao and Joao's best friend Sanket were left.

"Don't worry, re," Joao was saying. "Every restaurant has to have a bar in Goa. Half our blood is beer. Sanket has done a bartending course in Bangalore. We can use his services for free."

Ricardo laughed and Joao continued, "Go home re. It's late. Your papa must be worried. You have done your bit. We'll take care of everything else—you relax."

Joao and Sanket looked on as Ricardo waddled home in his tight formal pants and then smiled at each other.

The Blessed Man
Kiran Mahambre

Sitting at the door of his hut, Narayan gazed at the land ahead. Land? It was really just a stretch of rocks. But Narayan had been growing a sparse crop of paddy there. If there had been enough water, he would have reaped two harvests of grain here. He would have grown some vegetables too. Even without water, he wished that land was his.

Most of the villagers had gone to the city. The fields had been left fallow. Cows now ambled through the landlord's plantations. With no one to feed them, how else would they fill their bellies?

The landlord only came to collect his coconut crop. He didn't bother with planting new saplings. Who wants this village? For higher education or to run a business one needs to go to the city. Health facilities are better in the city. Utilities, entertainment, they are all in the city. There's nothing in this village.

There's really no point in blaming the youth. Their expectations are high. They have an intellectual hunger. How will that be satiated in the village? Yet...

Narayan felt restless. His son wanted to go to the city to study. There was no point in stopping him. Why stop him? He was smart. He studied with great interest. But Narayan had always been drawn to the earth.

He longed to plant trees on the land in front of his house. He could picture clusters of trees on the embankment at the side. He would mentally tick off the names of the trees there. Flowering trees, fruit bearing trees, trees that would yield rich timber, medicinal trees ...

He shook his head. In the first place, the land belonged to the landlord. The water source too was at some distance. Only the monsoon crop could be grown here.

Narayan sat there in a dreamlike daze. Images of a ripened field came to his eyes. Great trees standing all around the golden field. Huge stacks of harvested grain ... He could see the threshing in progress, winnowed grain being filled into sacks. What a lovely sight!

Everyone complained that no one was ready to work in the fields. The workers are too costly, there is no value for the harvested grain ... and everything depends on the rain. Sometimes, just when you have planted the seed, down come torrents of rain. The seed is washed away and has to be planted all over again.

Sometimes the rain just shuts its eyes and pours on, and the grain rots. At times, the rains don't come at the right time. Swarms of hoppers attack the crop and the rice stalks fall over. If the rain is not enough, the grain doesn't fill out ... there's mostly chaff.

With no water source, all the effort goes to waste.

Yet, Narayan longed for the earth. He dreamt of lush fields. He would be delighted to see a sprouting seed in the ground. He would see the vegetable patch blooming in the rains and forget about his leaking thatched hut. More than

The Blessed Man

eating the fruit of the trees he had planted, just the sight of them gave him great joy. That fulfilled him.

Narayan felt irritated with himself. "I just sit and think of all this," he mumbled. "If this land could yield anything, why would the landlord have left it barren?" The landlord would water and grow some patches on his land for as long as his well water lasted.

Narayan's son had finished his SSC exams. He was a smart lad. He should study further, that's what the schoolteacher said. His wife thought her son should go to the town for higher studies and further employment.

But Narayan wished his son would study agriculture, to develop ways to make a fallow field come to life. Perhaps he could learn how to conserve the water that would run off during the monsoons, and use it to harvest crops in the summer. He could even conserve the trees of the forests.

The ranjani tree that bore bunches of tiny bluish purple flowers, the huski shrubs with dull green fruits, vag-chapko flowers ... where would one get such beauty? Where would we get the fragrance of the suringa and onvall trees? And the wild lokhann ... when a bunch of those fine white flowers bloomed, the whole forest filled with heavenly scent. Could the perfumes brought from Kuwait match these flowers? But no one cared to preserve these trees.

Some grow son-chafo trees. The nag-chafo tree, however, is nowhere to be seen. Agasti flowers, mandir flowers ... earlier people used to grow these to offer the flowers to God, but now even their names are unfamiliar. No one loves to grow trees any more. The santan tree that blooms during Diwali fills the whole village with fragrance, and looks beautiful to the beholder too. But people don't want such trees. It is now fashionable to grow shrubs and cacti in vases.

How much money would be needed to send the boy to the city, Narayan wondered. Striving to achieve dreams did not mean that practical needs could be set aside.

He had saved some money to buy the land. Laws were being passed where you could now own the land that you tilled. Even if it was barren land. Hopefully the landlord would sell all this barren land cheaply to him.

Foolish hopes! Yet Narayan had collected his earnings over the years in the hope of buying that land. He placed half of his savings in his son's hands and said, "Learn well, son. But find some way to grow crops on barren land. Study the arts of the fields and the forests."

The son was overwhelmed. "Father, I too have been thinking of the same thing. I will study agriculture." Narayan felt he had touched the sky in his happiness.

Years passed and according to the new Mundkar Act, the time came for the land to be transferred to the tiller. Narayan humbly told the landlord, "Bhatkara, you know the land in front of my house is rocky. There isn't any water available to even grow vegetables. Please see if you can give it to me at a low price. I will be grateful."

The landlord was a benevolent man. When the other landlords had driven Narayan away out of fear of the tenancy laws, it was this gentleman who had given him a place to build his hut.

He contemplated Narayan's request. "It is true that the land is rocky. If it could be cultivated I myself would have done so all these years. If this man can succeed there, let him reap its fruit. These lands have made us wealthy. Now we cannot work on them. Let those who desire to work on them do so. If we sell to builders, we will make money, but we will not be able to repay what we owe this land. I only hope Narayan himself doesn't sell it off to the builders later."

The Blessed Man

The landlord sold the land to Narayan for a nominal price. Narayan paid out all the money he had in the bank and got the land in his name.

As the paperwork of the land transfer was getting done, his son too finished his final exams and returned home. He had to now get a job. Their hut was still the same old hut. There was no money left in the bank. And there wasn't much hope for the crop. The rains were approaching and Narayan was not sure of earning any daily wages himself either. On one hand, Narayan felt the joy of finally owning the land, but on the other hand lay the worry of tomorrow.

Narayan, his wife and son ate their dinner in silence. Storm clouds had gathered. Peals of thunder could be heard in the distance. The thunder gradually came closer. It began to rain. Narayan, who had been keenly listening to the rain in the dark, eventually closed his eyes and fell asleep.

"Boom!"

There was an ear-splitting and almost head-splitting explosion outside.

All three woke up with a shock. It was pouring very heavily. They could not figure out what had broken, or what had fallen around them. It was impossible to go out in the torrential rain. The three of them remained inside, trembling.

"Lightning must have struck somewhere," said Narayan.

It kept raining till dawn. As the sun rose, the showers stopped. Narayan and his son stepped out of their hut. They walked on and reached the middle of the rocky land, now their own. They stared at the ground in disbelief. A deep crater had formed where the lightning had struck and was now half filled with bubbling water.

Originally written in Konkani as 'Purushsya Bhagyam'. Translated by José Lourenço.

Tulsi and Tessika

Ahmed Bunglowala

Laxman Naik had retired all of three months ago from his monotonous job as an executive engineer with the PWD's water department. In the thirty-three years of his stifling—but 'lucrative'—work life Laxman had never been called upon to have any ideas or opinions of his own, which suited him fine. He didn't have much in the way of ideas or opinions that he wanted to express, anyway. Except, maybe, about the freshness of the fish he bought every morning from the local market. He was quite content carrying out the orders of his superiors, always particular that the paper work was immaculate in his clean and legible handwriting.

Now that he had retired he had no more 'orders' to carry out except from his wife Tulsi, who liked a good rubdown, on most days, before she went to sleep after a long day of cooking, cleaning and gossiping with the neighbours. He didn't always feel up to it but a few veiled threats from her that tomorrow could be a day without home-cooked 'fish curry rice' would usually galvanise him into some hands-on action. Just the mere thought of a *day* without his wife's fish curry rice was completely unnerving to him.

In his second month of retirement Laxman made quite a precipitous decision in his life. He wanted to see parts of Goa he had never laid eyes upon and in the process check out how the staple diet of the small state tasted outside the confines of his own home. He was also curious to unravel what the tourists *saw* in Goa; why this fatal attraction?

When he broached the idea to his wife that night—putting some extra effort into the rubdown—she was horrified. "There's nothing to see in Goa but half-naked tourists, Lamanis and those fishermen and construction workers from Karnataka and Orissa!" she whined. But for once he stood his ground. He tried to explain to her, in melodious Konkani—which he spoke with the slightest trace of a stutter—that the fishermen and construction fellows were here on the invitation of the Goan patrons who were too lazy and self-indulgent to get their own hands dirty. Except while eating their late lunches and dinners, delayed by a fond indulgence of feni, whiskey or beer. She understood what he was saying but sulked, nevertheless. He promised to bring her 'some nice things' from his travels—though he had absolutely no clue what he would get for her.

A bona fide Goan wanting to discover Goa was fraught with interesting possibilities; maybe unconsciously he was seeking a purple patch at this late stage in his life.

Secretly, Tulsi was quite relieved by her husband's decision. The last thing she wanted was for him to be hanging around the house the whole day. That would be stifling, she thought. On a more practical level, she rejoiced at the idea of keeping her sex life alive with her secret lover in Saligao. Not a soul had got a whiff of her illicit affair, except her sister who shared her lover with Tulsi. A neat sisterly arrangement. In the land of the *Kamasutra* such things still happen, despite the mouldy screen of Indian middle-class hypocrisy.

For the last thirty-odd years of his existence Laxman had led a very predictable life. Leaving his house in a fishing and farming vaddo in Nerul on his Honda scooter on the dot of nine am and bolting his office in Porvorim—as if it were on fire—on the dot of six pm, he would reach home at six-forty pm to eat a fried snack with tea which his wife would invariably keep ready for him. What he did in his small cubicle at the Public Works Department was something rather difficult to fathom. He would pore over files, rearrange the official circulars in the ring binder; order fried mirchi and tea to be brought to him twice in the day and would receive and make calls on his landline and mobile. Most of the calls he received were in the nature of complaints—faulty water meters not replaced, new water connections still pending, requests for disconnection of water supply ignored. He would listen to the complainants patiently and at the end of it offer his well-rehearsed, standard response: "I will get it done tomorrow." The seasons would change—the hot and sultry summer to a wet and torrid monsoon—and his promised 'tomorrow' would still be on hold. His phones kept ringing.

When he retired he was strangely relieved that the phone calls would now be the headache of his younger successor, a man he disliked and whom he thought unworthy of the important post he was vacating. At his farewell party his bosses and colleagues had mouthed fulsome praise about his 'long and dedicated' service to the people of Goa. Laxman almost believed the spiel to be true. He told his wife, that night, that his bosses and colleagues sounded heartbroken because of his leaving. She just shrugged her shoulders. "They have to say these things. They don't mean a word of what they ramble on at these farewell functions," she said with a soothing intonation in her voice. "Come, I have made your favourite fish." He had sentimental tears in his eyes as he started to eat his wife's elaborate meal, which she had painstakingly cooked to soften the blow of his last day in office. "From tomorrow," she cajoled him, "you are a free bird."

For a government employee, Laxman had shown considerable entrepreneurial flair. He had bought two scooters which he hired out to British, Russian or Scandinavian tourists in the high season by the week or month at exorbitant and sometimes fanciful rates. On his wife's prodding—who was a good fifteen years younger than him—he had also got around to converting one of the rooms in their red-tiled house into a guest room for firangi tourists. No Indians, they had decided—too loud, too demanding, too Indian. The only time they had made an exception—and 'regretted' the decision—was when they had rented their guest room to a tall, smiling, attractive, mysterious and ostensibly single Indian woman in her early thirties. She had got the bachelors, husbands and old widowers in the neighbourhood so worked up that Tulsi had decided to take some decisive action. She asked her lady guest to summarily move out, much to the secret regret of her husband and the other men in the neighbourhood. This sudden development came as a rude break in their fantasies and their daily time-pass of chatting her up to see any signs of interest on her part. She was not interested in the locals. She was a smooth hustler—beyond their range and comprehension.

So in the end, it had all added up to a nice egg nest for the Naiks and the fact that they had no children had made them that much more solvent and secure—no 'market-rate' dowry, no fancy college fees, no expensive electronic gizmos, no budget-draining holidays.

On a cool day in November—when a steady influx of

cheap chartered flights with their dubious dregs of penny-pinching tourists were landing at Dabolim airport—Laxman Naik decided to start his exploration of Goa. He had been reading up on Goa in the well-thumbed copies of *The Lonely Planet* and *The Rough Guide* left behind by their firangi guests. He realised he had spent so little time in Panjim that he hardly knew the capital of the state, except for the occasional shopping trips to the Municipal Market with his wife on Sundays.

The city grew on him on his frequent visits. The Mandovi river promenade, Mahavir Garden, the quaintly painted heritage buildings of Fontainhas; on the outskirts, Old Goa with its worn out charms and Divar Island in a time warp of its own. However, the brief ferry crossing from Betim to Panjim and vice versa was always the high point of his day. He felt a child-like thrill as the noisy engines roared to life. The panoramic views of the crossing stirred vague urges in him to write down his experiences and send it to a local paper for possible publication. Of course, he never got down to it. The good old habit of procrastination always got the better of him. On the ferry, he always made it a point to notice the people who would be making a last-ditch effort to get on to it. In a way it exemplified the kind of risk taking he had eschewed all his life.

On some days he would try to get his wife interested in his travelogue as he dutifully gave her a massage in their secluded, dimly lit house facing a wide expanse of community fields—miraculously still out of the reach of rapacious developers who were hell bent on transforming Goa into a faceless and soulless concrete jungle. She was hardly interested in his wanderings and would ask him the same question every time: *What did you eat today?* That particular day he had eaten and enjoyed a fish meal in one of the small eateries, in one of the narrow bylanes of Panjim and had ordered an extra plate of rice to polish off the remainder of his fish curry. "Nothing like yours," he declared. "Liar," she retorted. "A little more pressure on the lower back."

After he had had his fill of Panjim, he took the first dolphin trip of his life with a small group of Brits, followed by a visit to the flea market of Anjuna. He look a car trip to Palolem without any agenda and sat the whole day at a beach shack drinking beer and eating rawa fried kingfish. The shack—Tony's Bar & Grill—was listed in one of the travel bibles which partly explained the premium prices on the menu. For once in his life he didn't mind the extravagance. He felt a sense of freedom, like his wife had predicted on that fateful last day at office. On his second pint of beer, Laxman struck up a conversation with a middle-aged foreigner sitting at the next table, staring fixedly at the sea. It turned out that the taciturn man was a Roma gypsy with no permanent address. "No one wants us for long," he said gloomily. "We live on the fringes of civilisation; making a living from what people throw away." Laxman was intrigued. What a contrast, he thought, to his thirty-three years with the PWD!

One December morning Laxman bought himself a fancy pair of sun shades and a big straw hat and headed out to Ponda to visit a spice farm known for its Saraswat cooking—attracting many agenda-driven tourists. The tour guide to the spice garden was a bit tipsy and kept repeating things and mixing up the names of spices. Laxman's eyes, however, kept wandering in the direction of a blonde who was evincing a deep interest in the fascinating world of spices. When the Saraswat spread was ready to be served on banana leaves, Laxman manoeuvred himself to a place next to the same attractive Russian-looking woman. When everyone was seated around the big table, the waiters got busy plying their guests with an assortment of fish, prawns, mussels, vegetables, rice, lentils and pickles—much to the ooh-aah amazement of the mixed group of foreign tourists who were quickly downing the food with long gulps of beer.

"Too chilly?" Laxman tentatively asked the thirty-something woman sitting inches away from him.

"Noo, not at all," she said looking squarely at him with her startling blue-grey eyes. "I like zit spicy in India. Goa very spicy and cool." She chuckled.

"You coming from Russia?" Laxman probed, feeling more confident.

"Not Russia, Uzbekistan." She took a generous mouthful of prawns and rice laced with the fiery Saraswat pickles.

Not wanting to sound ignorant, Laxman changed the subject, "You travel alone?"

"Yees, noo. I have my *Lonely Planet* with me always! You come from Goa?"

"Goan from Goa," he said proudly. "My name is Laxman."

"I am Tessika."

"Your country beautiful?" Laxman asked, gulping down a cupful of solkadi, tangy kokum juice laced with spices.

"Yees. But no sea shore. We are a doubly landlocked country."

Doubly, Laxman wondered. "You come to Goa for sea shore?"

"Yees. Also for dancing and vodka." She laughed again. An easy, confident laugh.

"Try some of this," he said pointing to her untouched solkadi. "Good for digestion and complexion."

She took his advice and drank up the solkadi. "Very tasty, better than beer," she commented. Laxman gave her a big Made-in-Goa smile—part leer, part charm, part innocence.

When he reached home that evening, he was feeling very happy with himself. The finely balanced Saraswat food and his chance meeting with the blonde Uzbek woman, who had shown an easy and comfortable disposition towards him, had boosted his libido and self esteem. He made love to his wife that night with renewed enthusiasm, and post coitus decided to make a serious attempt to get rid of his prominent Goan belly.

Soon his wife and the neighbours in his village noticed a marked difference in Laxman's demeanour. He looked happier, trimmer and more self-confident. He took long walks, ate in moderation and looked forward to the 'vegetarian days' in the week, persuading his wife to make his favourite vegetables: red pumpkin, bitter gourd and white gourd. He gave up his constant hankering for fish curry rice for which he was soundly and persistently ridiculed in his blinkered neighbourhood. He bought himself a book on the birds of Goa to educate himself on the avian species of the state; one morning he made a nesting shelter—improvised from an empty five-litre plastic can—and hung it on a tree outside his house. He decided to be more useful around the house doing routine maintenance jobs which he had characteristically kept putting off. He even brought his wife a belated present. A choker made of burnished metal, from the Tibetan market in Calangute. She was quite taken aback by his choice.

In all this, he made it a fetishist ritual to ride the Betim-Panjim-Betim ferry as often as he could in the bracing winter months. He even caught it once—the last ferry for the day—in an athletic sprint, just in the nick of time. *Paulo re*, he muttered to himself. I made it.

Tulsi and Tessika were waiting, arm-in-arm, at the Betim jetty to drive him home in a red hatchback—Tessika's new acquisition, just whizzed out of the showroom. She had moved into the Naiks' guest room, a week ago, with her famous chuckle— "I like it when I live in Goa with a Goan family. It feels *soo* good."

As he was getting into the car, Laxman noticed that Tessika was wearing the choker he had bought for Tulsi. It looked beautiful on her long, poised Uzbek neck. He threw a questioning glance at his wife. She gave him a sweet smile of complicity.

The Little Pink Purse

Giselda Menezes

God! Please don't let me be late again, thought Julia as she limped hurriedly towards the bus stop. She stole a quick glance at her watch and groaned nervously. It was past eight-thirty in the morning. She was already running late and her broken sandal worsened her plight. She contemplated picking it up and making a dash for it, but as sedate office goers filled the street she decided against it.

So she limped along, her dignity intact, only to see her bus leaving, a short distance away from the stop. Julia's heart sank. She just couldn't afford to be late today!

Suddenly, something inside her snapped. "Hey, wait!" she yelled, as she picked up her sandals and made a run for it. But it was too late. Julia watched helplessly as the bus raced off. She had missed it by an inch, literally!

She sat down to catch her breath and thought quickly. The train station was just a few minutes away. If she hurried, she could catch the next train which was due in twenty minutes. She would still get to the office a bit late, but at least it would be faster than catching the next bus. Julia sighed; this was just going to be one of those days!

A little while later, Julia settled down on a platform seat as she waited for the train to arrive. She placed her bag on the seat beside her and bent down to examine her sandal. She tied the broken strap into a quick knot and sighed. That quick-fix would suffice until she got to a cobbler. She sat up straight and checked her watch. She had about fifteen minutes to go before the train arrived. She fished out her reading glasses and settled down to read her latest pick, by Jeffery Archer. Right now, the novel was the best remedy for her nerves.

Having purchased his ticket, Andy picked up his duffel bag and headed towards the platform. He had about ten minutes before the train arrived. He hoped he would find some interesting company on the journey. He hated travelling alone, but he had no option this time.

He looked around, hoping to spot a vacant seat. As he scanned the platform, his eyes fell upon a young lady who seemed to be engrossed in some book. She looked a bit familiar, but he couldn't recall having met her before. He noticed the empty seat beside her and smiled to himself. That appeared to be a good option! She seemed like a regular, and her companionship might come in handy along the way.

"Excuse me, miss? Is this seat taken?" A male voice interrupted her reading. Julia looked up with a slight start. She had been engrossed in her book.

"May I?" asked the young man in front of her, gesturing towards her bag on the adjacent seat.

"Sorry," mumbled Julia, picking up her bag and placing it on her lap. She scowled inwardly. Did he just *have* to bother her? Couldn't he find anywhere else to sit? There were so

The Little Pink Purse

many empty seats around, but he *had* to pick this one.

She watched quietly as he put down his rather heavy-looking duffel bag and sat beside her. She observed him from the corner of her eye, pretending to be engrossed in her book. He was a tall, dark-haired youth, clean shaven and neatly dressed. But there was something about him that made her feel uneasy. Maybe it was just the bold manner in which he had approached her. She continued to read, hoping he didn't sense her nervousness.

Andy studied her silently. Hmm. Not a very friendly contender, he thought to himself.

"Do I know you from somewhere?" he asked after a few moments of silence.

"Yeah! I'm a supermodel!" she replied with a slight smirk. "And we usually aren't too friendly."

He laughed, "I'm sorry. That *did* sound like some corny old pick-up line. But you really do look terribly familiar."

Julia shrugged and went back to her book, but was unable to concentrate. She really didn't want to befriend a stranger. There were so many awful stories in the news these days. The city was not as safe as it used to be. She forced herself to appear composed. She could not let him realise she was afraid. That would just make her seem like an easy target and she would not let that happen.

"A Jeffery Archer fan, are you?" he persisted, nodding toward her novel.

"What business of yours is that?" She snapped back. Why couldn't he just leave her alone?

He seemed astonished at her reply. "Well! That was a first time." He muttered with a wry smile. Julia blushed slightly. Maybe she was just over-reacting. She studied him again. He did seem okay. But she wasn't taking any chances. She turned back to her book.

Andy wondered if he should just leave her alone. She was not as friendly as she appeared! But her unwillingness to engage in casual conversation seemed to challenge his ego. A few moments later he decided to give it another shot. "Do you always read like that?" he asked.

She turned and scowled at him but said nothing.

"I mean backwards," he explained. "Do you always read backwards? You were at page 75 when I got here and you are now at 55." His smile was mischievous now.

Julia felt her face flush. She had been only absent-mindedly flipping the pages since he had parked himself next to her and his sharp observation worried her even further. "Look mister," she began, "I've already had a terrible day so far without you having to make it any worse. I've missed my bus, I'm going to be late to work and I'm probably not going to make the best first impression on my new boss. The last thing I need now is to befriend some stranger who will probably just run away with my money!" she blurted, all in one breath.

Andy was momentarily speechless. He stared at her wide-eyed with amusement. "Well," he said finally, "That's a real nice impression you have formed about me! I didn't realise I came across as a mugger! Guess I'll have to work a little more on my appearance."

"Listen mister, I just ..."

"No, it's okay. I understand," he picked up his bag and slung it over his shoulder. "Sorry to have bothered you, miss. You have a nice day," he said to her as he strode off casually and disappeared into the crowd.

Moments later, the train pulled into the station. Julia fought her way through the crowd to a vacant aisle seat in a compartment. She settled down and pushed the stray strands of hair off her face. Phew! Thank God she didn't have to deal with this stampede every morning!

She could feel tiny rivulets of sweat run down her spine. She was feeling so sticky and sweaty, she was sure she'd be reeking by the time she reached the office. She would just have to freshen up in the ladies room.

She rummaged through her bag and dug out her pink purse. She checked her ticket and leaned back in her seat, satisfied. But her tranquillity was soon shattered by a painfully familiar voice.

"Well! I was hoping I'd find better company in the train than I did on the platform!"

Julia's heart sank as she turned to face the speaker. If only she had noticed him before, she wouldn't have made the terrible mistake of sitting beside him. She frowned, "Maybe today just isn't your lucky day!" she told him.

"Or yours!" he grinned.

Julia grinned back unable to suppress herself. Today *had* been a rotten day and it wasn't showing any signs of getting better!

"Wait a minute!" he blurted suddenly. "You aren't stalking me, are you?" he asked accusingly, in a rather icy tone that sent a shiver down her spine. He gave her a cold, hard stare and she stared back bewildered, "I ... But you ..."

He raised his hands up in the air in mock surrender and laughed heartily. "I'm sorry! I just *had* to see that expression!"

Julia smiled weakly. But she was far from amused. She could feel her heart pounding. Images from the thriller flick *Red Eye* danced before her eyes. Who was this guy? What did he want? What if he held her hostage? But, what could he want from *her*? She shuddered. She didn't intend to stick around and find out. Her heart raced. She had to get away from him. Her head suddenly felt very light and her legs felt like jelly. She could feel beads of sweat forming on her brow.

"Are you okay, miss?" he interrupted her thoughts.

"Huh?"

"You don't look too good."

Julia stared at him. "I'm okay. Just a little motion-sickness, I guess." She took a deep breath and tried to calm down.

"Maybe you'd prefer to sit by the window?"

"No thanks!" she almost growled at him. The last thing she needed was to be trapped in that corner.

"I just thought ..."

"I'll be fine," she cut him off. "I just need to shut my eyes for a while."

He opened his mouth to reply, but didn't say anything. Julia heaved a silent sigh of relief. She shut her eyes and began assessing her options. She just had to get away from this guy! Maybe she could get off at the next station and catch a cab from there. It would be an expensive option, but at least it would get her out of this mess. She tried to relax till then.

Julia wove her way through the crowd, her heart thumping away. She hoped he hadn't noticed her leave. He had been asleep when the train pulled into the station and she had tiptoed away, off the train. She quickened her pace, only to trip on her sandal.

Damn! Don't give way now, she prayed silently as she glanced over her shoulder. Her heart sank at what she saw. Her stalker was steadily weaving his way through the crowd and he was headed towards her. She panicked. She was right about him after all! She hastened her steps and prayed she would find a cab soon. Just then, she felt the

The Little Pink Purse

knot snap. *Damn damn damn!* She dragged her torn sandal along as she made her way to the exit, not daring to look behind. Her eyes scanned the exit for a taxi.

Only a few metres away from the exit gate, she felt a heavy hand on her shoulder. Her heart skipped a beat and she spun around to face her tormentor again.

"Look here mister," she yelled at him as ferociously as she could. "Just leave me alone!"

"Listen, you ..."

"You just stay away!" she hissed, stepping back from him. Her warning seemed to have the desired effect and he froze in his tracks. She turned and hurried away but he sprinted after her.

She stopped and whirled around to face him again, her eyes blazing. "Stop following me," she warned, clutching in her hand the weapon she had dug out from her bag. She *would* use it if she had to.

"Look miss," he said finally, looking quite infuriated. "All I was saying was ..."

But she didn't wait to hear him out. Julia aimed the pepper can right at the man's face and sprayed its contents straight into his deep brown eyes.

"Ow, ow, ow ..." he hollered, grabbing her hand as he staggered forward in pain and shock. With all the force she could muster, Julia swung her handbag straight into his face, adding to his agony. He let go of her hand and clutched his eyes. "I can't see," he cried. "What the hell have you done?"

As soon as she was free from his grasp, Julia dashed towards the exit. She was trembling all over and her hands were cold. She had dropped her glasses in the scuffle but she dared not stop to pick them up. She had no idea how long the effect of the spray would last; she had to get away as fast as possible. Luckily, there was a taxi waiting just outside the exit and she dashed into it. She glanced over her shoulder as the cab drove off. Her assailant was standing bewildered, amidst curious bystanders. He seemed to have recovered from the spray and was staring at her rather strangely.

Andy's teary eyes felt like they were on fire. This was the first time anything like this had happened to him! As she sped off in the taxi, he had recognised her face. Now he realised why she had seemed so familiar! He had recognised her only without her glasses. He picked up the little pink purse he had dropped during the struggle and grinned, despite his smarting eyes. He slung his duffel bag over his shoulder and headed to the station washroom to rinse his face. Then he called the office to say he would be a little late.

"Shirley! What did I miss?" whispered Julia as she sank into the chair next to her friend.

She had reached the office ten minutes late and, after a quick trip to the ladies room, had rushed to the conference hall. Almost all her other colleagues had already gathered in the room and were anxiously awaiting their boss' address.

"Nothing much," yawned Shirley. "The new boss just called to inform Mr Thomas that he'd be a bit late."

"Wow! Late on the first day itself!"

"Sounds like your kind of guy," Shirley teased.

Julia scowled, "Very funny Shirley! You wouldn't believe what a dreadful morning I've had. And I even lost my favourite little pink purse."

"What happened?"

"There was this guy on the train ..."

Just then, the door to the conference room opened and in walked a tall, dark-haired youth, clean shaven and neatly dressed in a white full-sleeved shirt and a blue tie.

Julia stared, open mouthed. This had to be a horrible dream. This just couldn't be happening, she thought mournfully! She slouched down into her seat, praying he would not notice her. But, as if he had read her mind, he turned in her direction and his eyes met hers. Julia flushed when she noticed they were still red from her brutal attack! And, in his left hand he was holding a bright pink purse!

She barely heard Mr Thomas: "Everybody ... Mr Andrew Martins ... your new boss!"

The Legend of the Rakhonddar

Celina Amaral e Cota

The term *Rakhonddar* probably derives from *Rakhno*, meaning shepherd or guardian in Konkani, the mother tongue of Goa. *Gonvlli* signifies milkman: *gonvllis* belong to a tribe that rear buffaloes and cows for milk, which they sell to local villagers. The milkmen live a simple life in rural surroundings. Their dwellings are generally near fields or forests or in the vicinity of lakes, since they need water for their cattle or goats.

My story dates back many years, fifty or more? Nobody knows.

The Guardian lives on the top of the mountain, according to the local folk, the mountain from which flows the fascinating Dudhsagar Waterfall, which means 'Sea of Milk.' This waterfall is known to all, thanks to its imposing beauty, a true gift of nature to the people of Goa. The Guardian comes down every night to the railway station, according to local lore, sliding gently down the waterfall, which cascades like a white sheet and forms a small lake close to the railway station. Here the Guardian boards the train and only alights

The Legend of the Rakhonddar

at Chandor to go to the famous Rai Tollem, which means Lake of the King, situated in the village of Curtorim. This lagoon is yet another beautiful gift of nature: a water-body surrounded by green fields as far as the eye can see, attracting birds of every colour and species. The birds chirp all day on the branches of trees swaying in the breeze and are reflected in the serene waters of the lake. The lake abounds in fish, particularly the tasty 'pintoll'.

When the train approaches the lake, say the local people, the engine driver slows down and blows his whistle. This happens after midnight. The whistle is a sign that the Guardian has alighted from the train. According to some, he steps out of the train and into the lake. Some say he takes the trip from Dudhsagar just once a year and travels all the way to the station at the town of Vasco da Gama. But the general belief is that he comes every night, arriving after midnight and leaving back for Dudhsagar by dawn. The Rai Tollem lake is breathtaking, and our story unravels here.

Five friends decided to go on a hunting trip in the woods near Curtorim village. These are thick woods, difficult to penetrate. In places, not even the sunlight can break through, and anyone walking through the woods even in broad daylight might think it is dark night. The place is teeming with dangers like wild animals, reptiles and deadly insects, particularly the red and black ants. The men carried guns, sticks and choppers besides their packed lunch and water, as they expected to be away for long hours. They walked many miles with no luck, they were unable to catch any prey. Exhausted, they sat in a clearing in the woods and shared their food and their bottles of their favourite drink, the local 'urrack'. One of them drank so much that he could not even stand on his feet. It was late, so they decided to rest for a while. The moon shone its silvery light, the leaves of the bushes seemed like so many pearls, and the breeze rustled softly by. Having rested, the men went their way, now not too steady on their feet. One of them fell and fractured his arm. Nothing could be done but bear the pain and soldier on.

They walked for another two hours until they came to a clear stream. Tired, they rested by the bank of the stream and refreshed themselves with cold water, a soothing balm after their exhausting journey. They were now ready to go on, when they noticed that one of the five was missing. What were they to do? Go back? That was too long a trek, and their two hours' walk had drained them of all energy. They decided to return to the village and conspired to say nothing to the wife of the friend who had disappeared. As they were about to move ahead, they suddenly heard a nasal voice warning them that they would be punished if they failed to help the friend they were missing. "Beware," rasped the voice, "punishment awaits you!" Still they ran, like men possessed, down steep paths paved with sharp stones and thorns that tore at their feet. They were oblivious to pain and ran as if a ghost was pursuing them.

The unfortunate wife of the man who had disappeared had spent a sleepless night, and she and her son were awaiting him at the house of one of the friends. Mother and son were stunned to see that the returning friends were only four. A terrible moment for them! Every dark thought crossed the woman's mind—"Had he been killed by a wild animal?" The friends found it difficult to face her and give her a reasonable explanation. Finally the boldest of them blurted out that her husband had vanished as they were resting by the bank of a river. Another piped up that he had gotten completely drunk and was cursing obscenely. Yet another commented that he must have been abducted by the mountain 'Guardian'. The poor woman, crazy with anxiety, did not know where to turn. She said to her son, "My boy, let's go and look for your father, we cannot abandon him. These men, do they call themselves his friends?"

The two ran like the wind, hardly aware which way they were heading. They found themselves in a dense forest and collapsed at the foot of a massive tree. Half-dead with fatigue, they fell asleep. How long were they there? Hours, days, weeks, months or years, who knows? When they awoke from a deep sleep, they felt rejuvenated. As they opened their eyes, they were startled to see a man of exceptional height, tough and muscular in build and dressed in a pure white tunic and a red turban. In his hand he held a huge staff with small bells hanging all along the length of it. They thought he looked horrible, with eyes burning like coals.

The woman and the boy were terrified to come face to face with such a creature; but the Guardian— that is who he was—said to them, "Don't be afraid, I'm the good spirit of the forest. I've come to assure you that your husband is safe and sound." Amazed, the lady wanted to know how her husband had survived without food or water for so long. The Guardian replied, "I fed him the fruit and the juices that this forest offers. I'm the good spirit of the forest. I don't like to hurt anyone, but if anyone insults me, I do not spare him, I have him severely punished." The woman stammered, "Why was my husband punished, then?" The Guardian said, "I was around when he was swearing and using absolutely foul language. I hate all that." The woman begged, "Oh, Spirit of the Forest, will you please forgive him?" The Guardian answered, "Certainly, but he must first apologize." The woman wept and cried out, "I'll do whatever I can, just tell me what to do, and where I can find him." The Guardian said to the woman, "You are a good woman, so I'll help you out. I shall give you a magical stone which sparkles brightly and will guide you to the spot where your husband is hiding." The woman fell at his feet, full of gratitude. The Guardian said, "Take this bag too, it contains fruit to slake your hunger and thirst." Saying this, he vanished from their sight.

The woman and her son were stunned; they had no choice but to obey the instructions of the Guardian. They set out on their way and walked for a few hours until they came to a stream of clear water. Suddenly the woman felt drops of water sprinkling on her. She thought it was going to rain. She looked at the sky but it was clear and blue. But she noticed something amazing—on top of a tall tree sat her husband. He had seen them and was now weeping. It was his tears that fell like raindrops on her. She called out to him, but he just sat there still and silent.

What were they to do now? The boy began to plan. He could not climb the tree, it was too tall and the thick trunk offered no branches that might help him up. But they had taken along a large knife and a small axe to defend themselves. They now went in search of bamboo trees. They cut them up and fashioned a long ladder and tied it to the tree with creepers. The boy clambered up the tree swiftly. He spoke to his father, but the man would not respond. From down, the woman kept imploring her husband, "Ask God for forgiveness, man, and if you've offended anyone else with your curses, ask them too." Then the man opened his eyes and with the help of his son, came down the ladder to the ground. He shook uncontrollably, but could not utter a word. The woman pulled him into her arms and they all wept with joy. The man tried to explain what had happened, but all he could manage were incoherent sounds. Just then they heard the sound of hundreds of little bells. The Guardian reappeared. He had come to warn them never to cross him again with ugly curses and obscenities.

Fully rested, the man, the woman and their son returned to the village. But to their amazement, everything had vastly changed. Their own house looked more like a poor hut compared to their original home, and was in ruins. As they moved down the paths, they noticed that the houses were not the same as the ones they knew. They met an old man, bent at the waist and smoking a bidi, but they failed to recognize him. He was one of the four friends who had abandoned the man to his fate. But he did recognize them. He fell to his knees begging for forgiveness. And they all lived happily together ever after.

Such are the folk stories about the *Rakhonddar*, stories that are part of our ancient lore. There are many of them, all with a moral. This one, of course, admonishes the listener never to abandon a friend in need.

Originally written in Portuguese as 'A Lenda do Rakondar'. Translated by Isabel Santa Rita Vas.

The Girl in the Frame

Aldina Braganza e Gomes

All Giselle blabbered to Zubin for the week prior to boarding the Ratchi Rani, the Bombay-Goa steamer, had been about the things she would enjoy on her trip home.

At the top of the list was 'Visiting Avozinha'. Not because her grandmother prepared the most divine sausage pulao and recheado mackerels or because she had promised Giselle a surprise gift, but because Giselle genuinely loved her Avozinha.

For Giselle, Avozinha was the epitome of an empowered woman. She single-handedly managed the family estate and handled legal tribunals about disputes and settlements with her tenants. She would tell Giselle stories about life and pursuing dreams. "Even happiness is achieved only and only if you truly desire it," she would say. It was with such ideas that Giselle had come to Mumbai, to pursue her dreams of working at the World Health Organization.

A postgraduate degree from the Tata Institute of Social Sciences would help, Zubin had suggested, and since she had taken his advice, Zubin felt responsible for Giselle in Mumbai. He had even arranged for his friend's mother to send Giselle a *dabba* with fish curry and rice once a week, in the hope that she would miss home a little less.

She had met Zubin in her Sociology class three years ago, when his family had moved to Goa. She had found his strange views on religion and life very attractive and they had since been friends. There was no specific moment or situation when this friendship had turned to love. The closest incident Giselle would recollect later was an evening in November, when Zubin and she had gone to Mud Island. It may have been the sea gulls, the sunset or their proximity for the last couple of months, but as they held hands and played in the surf, Giselle had realised that life without Zubin in it would be very empty. When he dropped her back to her hostel later that evening, she had leaned forward, closed her eyes and they had shared their first kiss.

Giselle arrived at her grandmother's house in Goa and found Avozinha in the kitchen, multitasking as always, cooking pancakes stuffed with poached mangoes for tea, while also instructing Piedade to get the exact fluffiness for the wrap. It was Avozinha's special recipe. As soon as she caught sight of Giselle, she stretched her arms wide, her hands curled to avoid the gluey mango pieces from sticking to her grand-daughter.

They hugged.

Giselle noticed that her grandmother had lost weight and her eyes seemed sunken. Her mother had warned her about Avozinha's health.

Despite her age, Avozinha was carrying on, waiting for her son, Uncle Phillip, to return home from Portugal. She had lost almost all her old work force to the new Mundkar Act that granted land to the tiller-tenants, and now Piedade, her live-in house help, was her only help (sometimes they seemed like sisters), yet Giselle saw coconut copra and chillies kept out to dry in the rosangonn, the central courtyard. Mangoes lay buried in layers of hay to ripen and jackfruits were lined up against the wall of the storeroom.

"Years of practice make a habit," Avozinha would comment.

After tea she led Giselle to the sala de danse, a room that was evidence of the ostentatious life her ancestors had lived, and one which her grandmother would now open only for ceremonies and festivities. The wooden floor of this hall was supported by springs, designed for extra buoyancy that was a requisite of a good dance floor. The walls were decorated with paintings and huge mirrors framed in ivory that rested delicately on wooden hands; from the roof hung four chandeliers made with crystal imported from Belgium; the furniture was carved teak and rosewood, kept against the wall, with the exception of a round table that occupied the center.

On this table, neatly placed, was a camphor chest. It contained special crochet designs, handed across generations, since her great-great-grandmother's time.

"This is my special gift for you," Avozinha stated ceremoniously.

Giselle was astounded. She felt honoured that she had been chosen from amongst the other grandchildren to carry on the tradition.

"Wow! Thank you Avozinha," Giselle said, hugging her grandmother.

She opened the chest and let her hands feel the silk that wrapped the pieces before taking them out. She could not believe that this chest had just been gifted to her.

As a young girl, Giselle had been in awe of the intricacies of crochet; how a simple needle could disappear into the folds of Avozinha's hand almost effortlessly, as though engaged in a dance through which the most intricate patterns would come alive. She admired the simplicity; they were just chains, she realised, once she had her first lesson.

Each of these crochet pieces was a display of talent of the Costa women across three generations. They were exquisite! Roses, shoe-flowers, entire gulmohar trees with birds singing from their branches, bulbuls and peacocks, young girls with pretty frocks— patterns that flaunted every design she had seen before. The quality of thread, the finesse and the intricacy were overwhelming.

Avozinha had surprised her further with a second gift. Inside the box, Giselle discovered the most striking ivory satin silk thread and the reason for this ceremony.

"We are going to make a bed spread for your trousseau," Avozinha said sounding very excited.

This was not what Giselle had expected.

"I am not getting married so soon, Avozinha," Giselle said, doubtful that her family knew about her relationship with Zubin.

"Not tomorrow, but someday soon we shall have to find you someone," Avozinha said.

"Oh my God," Giselle thought. Zubin would have to come out of her closet sooner than she had anticipated.

Absent-mindedly Giselle had let her hands move further into the chest picking one design after another, each as beautiful as the next.

It was then that she felt something hard, under the silk. She lifted the silk cloth from the chest and saw a book; it looked as if it had been hidden, forgotten. Intrigued, she took the book and flipped through the pages which were brittle and yellow with age. She also noticed the ink had turned a pale grey ... Giselle realised it was someone's diary.

There were dates against the entry ... 27th June 1942.

Giselle recognised the handwriting. Her heart skipped a beat.

Giselle turned; she saw Avozinha sitting comfortably on the sofa, searching through a magazine for crochet patterns. Giselle read.

O lord I want to die ... The stink of liquor on his breath makes me sick. Every time he forces it hurts ... Every night I feel his roughness ... why did Piedade have to stop me ... What can I do ... O Jesus ... I am weak ... I want to die ...

Giselle could not read further. She closed the book.

Her head felt fuzzy, she had to hold the table for support.

"Avozinha?" she murmured.

"Yes?"

Giselle remained quiet. Her words choked in her throat.

"Such frankness ... was it possible?" Giselle wondered.

The stories Giselle had heard about her grandfather always revolved around the accolades of his ancestors. The only other thing Giselle knew about him was that granddad Costa had passed away young. Besides the photographs that hung on these walls, there was not much evidence of his existence. Giselle also knew that Avozinha was fiercely proud of the family name.

Giselle noticed Avozinha staring at her, waiting for her to say something, and automatically the diary went back into the chest once again, hidden under the silk.

"Are you okay?" Avozinha asked.

Giselle managed a smile.

"Can you bring the table runner from over there?" Avozinha said, pointing to the side table at the far end of the hall.

Giselle nodded.

Normally she would have skidded across the wooden floor, she loved the bounce, but today she dragged her feet across the hall.

Suddenly for Giselle, everything around her was a charade. She stopped in front of the cluster of photographs that hung on the wall. She saw men in tail coats and tall hats, and women in lace gowns posing with fans that were made from ostrich feathers; they all seemed profligate.

"How many such diaries lie hidden?" Giselle wondered.

She peered at the photographs.

"Are you alright?" Avozinha asked again.

"I am fine," Giselle replied.

She realised that one of the photographs was of her grandparents' wedding and she inquired about their ages.

"Your grandfather was thirty-seven and I was fourteen," Avozinha said.

"What?" Giselle screamed in utter disbelief.

She took the frame and held it in her hands.

"Fourteen, Avozinha? Fourteen!" Giselle repeated. "Was that even legal in your days?" Her voice reflected the disgust she had been feeling.

She sat on one of the chairs and sadly examined the young bride in the frame. Avozinha had moved to the table, her frail body bent over, checking the designs on the heirloom. She hadn't said a word.

Giselle took the frame closer to Avozinha.

"Look at this girl, Avozinha! She is young, so innocent and vulnerable ... I mean, look, see here ..." her fingers trailing the chest of the young girl in the frame, "She doesn't even have any breasts."

Avozinha had a faint smile on her face. She adjusted her spectacles with one hand, while the other hand held the frame, moving it to and fro, as if she was seeing the photograph for the first time.

"*Bekar tevoi* ..." Avozinha muttered, referring to a Konkani proverb on idle chatter, and kept the photograph on the table.

"Did you get the table runner?" She asked, ignoring Giselle's questions.

"Your husband could have been your father, you know," Giselle persisted, her voice still very angry and disturbed. "A reputed lawyer, how could he have believed in child marriage!"

"Your grandfather is dead, show some respect," replied her grandmother, her fingers drumming on the table.

But Giselle could not let this rest.

"There must have been some legality about it then," Giselle said.

The old woman turned to face her granddaughter, resting the small of her back against the rim of the carved table for support.

"And legal to you means you can do what you like?" Avozinha asked, her hands crossed in front of the chest, hoping that Giselle would back off.

"To choose, Avozinha ... You have the freedom to choose," Giselle said.

"And what about your choice? When do you want to get married? When you cross twenty-five? It will be difficult to get you a good man," Avozinha threw up her arms in desperation.

"Huh," exclaimed Giselle. She stomped back with the photograph and hung it on the wall. She needed to tell

Avozinha that the world had changed and today, women had a choice.

"So what makes you think I have not found myself a good man, Avozinha?" Giselle questioned.

"Have you?"

"Maybe."

"And who is this young man that I should get to know?"

Giselle hesitated. She moved to the side table and carefully removed the table runner from under the Chinese vase. She walked to Avozinha and handed her the runner.

"When he comes to Goa I shall bring him over to visit you," Giselle said gently with the hope that her grandmother would not react.

"You mean he is not Goan?"

"Yes."

"Yes he is Goan or Yes he is not Goan?" Avozinha insisted, a tinge of annoyance in her voice.

"Well, yes he is not a Goan," said Giselle, bracing for the reaction.

"What!"

Giselle could hear the shock in Avozinha's voice. She turned and moved to the wall. She stopped in front of the photographs of her ancestors, her grand aunts and grand uncles and their extended families. She knew which in-law was from which family and how they were related to her and she knew the inevitable question that would be asked next

"What family does he come from?"

"You mean caste or religion?" asked Giselle.

"I need to know ... our family has a reputation to maintain and so ..."

Giselle did not allow her grandmother to finish; she turned to face her.

"... And so you want me to compromise, Avozinha?"

"Marriage is a compromise. Families are important."

Giselle turned her attention back to the wedding photograph on the wall, as though comparing the relationship she had with Zubin with that of her grandparents.

"His name is Zubin and he respects me a lot and ... he is not a Catholic and ... as a matter of fact, as far as his caste goes, I have no idea," Giselle said and turned to face her grandmother once again.

There was a moment of silence before Avozinha's frozen frame moved. She saw Avozinha reach out for the sofa, gripping its arm for support as she sat down.

"You have no idea," Avozinha said, in a staccato voice. "Tell me how long has this been going on ... he is a Hindu, for God's sake ... a Hindu; they have hundreds of Gods and ... what does the Bible say? No other God than your own!"

"And I hope you still go to Church or has that too stopped?" Avozinha continued, her eyes moving up and down her granddaughter disgustedly, before peering at her face, perhaps to check if she had pierced her nose.

"God lives in your heart, Avozinha," Giselle found herself justifying. "Not in the church, or temple or mosque. And Zubin is a Parsi, not a Hindu ... a Parsi," Giselle explained.

"What's a Parsi?" Avozinha questioned, not hesitating to show her ignorance. Then her eyes widened and she began making the sign of the Cross.

"*Meu Deus* ... have you gone mad, Giselle Costa De Souza? Muslims! Even worse than the Hindus! Over my dead body!" Avozinha threatened Giselle.

"Avozinha, Zubin is a Parsi ... Zoroastrian ... and Parsis are not Muslims. What kind of a Catholic are you, accusing other religions ... and besides it doesn't matter ... Zubin and I don't believe in religions," Giselle retorted, realising a bit too late that was something that Avozinha did not have to hear.

Not now at least.

Giselle left the hall. She walked to the river that flowed behind the house; she noticed it was low tide and she would be able to wade across to the beach. She held her flip-flops in one hand and angled the other to balance her body in the sinking sand of the Baga river.

As the warm waters engulfed her feet Giselle wondered, "Did Avozinha walk on a lonely night into the swollen waters of this river hoping it would carry her away?"

At the click of a camera, Giselle realised, a moment too late, that she was being photographed by a drunken tourist.

"Bastard!" she screamed, shouting at the top of her voice.

It also dawned on Giselle that she would now have to tell her parents about Zubin.

Giselle walked to a more desolate part of the beach. She stood there, her hands in her pockets, facing the water, watching the shore.

As a young child, Avozinha had taught Giselle that the shore was a magic ground.

Giselle looked at her feet, they had disappeared into the shifting sand. She could hear Avozinha say, "See look, see, how they dissolve ... like magic". At night when they went swimming, Avozinha would rub her feet vigorously on the sand and the bioluminescent sea organisms would light up, as though she had given permission to the thousand stars that hid there to sparkle.

Giselle hoped for some magic.

She looked at the sky, slowly turning into an amber glow.

"The color of love," she could almost hear Zubin whisper in her ears. She missed him.

The spray of water mingled with the tears that rolled down her face.

Giselle returned long after the sun had set. She noticed the front balcony was dark and the main door open. She walked through, switched on some lights, and then went to the hall. Part of the heirloom and the rest of the materials lay scattered on the table beside the silk cloth.

She remembered the diary and searched for it in the chest.

The diary had disappeared.

She heard Piedade at a distance, informing everyone that dinner was served.

She went to Avozinha's room and found her sitting in the rocking chair, rocking herself gently, her hands trying to cover the diary on her lap. Her face was streaked with tears.

Giselle walked to her grandmother, reached out and gently wiped the tears from her face. Tenderly hugging the frail woman, she let her face rest on her bosom. With one hand she caressed the silver withered hair and with the other she gently removed the diary and kept it aside.

Them Bones

Tanvi Srivastava

Shanta Rodrigues was sitting on a wooden cane chair, arranging flowers in a bowl when the doorbell rang.

"Never a moment's peace," she said as she walked with some difficulty towards the apartment door. "*Yaaradu?*" Her anglicised Kannada rolled awkwardly against her palate.

"It is Ratna, Ajji. Krishnan madam sent me."

She opened the door to let in a slight, shadowy woman of perhaps forty. "The cleaning things are in the room beyond the kitchen. Over there!"

"Ma, can I have some cake?" interrupted Safia.

"Chee, no! It's not even ten o'clock." Shanta pulled the screaming bolt to a close. "Safia, what are you doing?"

Safia giggled from the dining table, a long strip of saliva lolling below her chin.

"Why can't you behave yourself? Wipe your mouth now." Shanta returned to her flowers as Ratna appeared with a wooden broom and pan. "No, no, start with the dusting first. The cloth is hanging on the balcony. Imagine, I bought these lilies just this morning. Already nothing but twigs. Oh, my knees."

"Can we have chicken for lunch, Ma?"

"Hmm?"

"Butter chicken? Yum." Safia's ragged curls rolled as she rubbed her belly. "From Delhi. Remember how Daddy took us to Copper Chicken."

"Copper Chimney. Button your sweater, it's getting chilly."

"Even Jhupu was there ... and ... and she had a bad tummy!" Safia clapped her hands in delight. "I love chicken, Ma. I love sucking on leg bones."

"Button your sweater."

"I don't want to."

"It's cold, Safi. Look outside, it's raining again."

The sky was a fat dimpled grey.

"No!" She pulled at the buttons of the undersized lilac sweater that Shanta had knitted almost fifteen years ago.

"You already have a cough. Do you want me to call Dr Seshadri? Aye, lift the books and clean behind them too!"

Shanta's face crumpled in annoyance as she observed the maid. Ratna was attempting to lift a precarious pile of books at the top of which rested a mouldy red Oxford dictionary. The dictionary fell, breaking its spine, and forgotten words and photographs streaked across the mosaic floor. Ratna bent down to pick up the scattered pages, her ragged sari falling off her shoulder, revealing the caterpillar of her own black-leathered spine.

A photograph of Jerome flashed before her eyes.

"Give that to me," said Shanta, flouncing her hands as she walked hurriedly towards Ratna. In the photograph, Jerome's gaunt face laughed back at her, the pink-tinted mountains of Nainital rising behind his shoulders. He had always loved to travel. Shanta felt the warmth of a smile spread across her face. She remembered their old Fiat and all the adventures and misadventures they had had. Without a destination or a thought. Life seemed endless then. Impossibly endless. They would dream and whisper into each others' ears; arched longings, sighs of life and love. He always told her they were meant to be, no matter what their families said. He flowed in her veins, in the whispers of her hair, between her lips. She slipped into his words and swirled into a lifetime of love.

She was married at twenty-one, he twenty-seven. He renounced his Catholicism, his father's auctioneering business, and his ancestry in Goa. Her family had never been too religious. Never too traditional. Yet, she too claimed to renounce it all for him. All that she wanted was him. All that she had was him. Nothing to lose but him.

He had always wanted children. Lots of children. Two boys and a girl at least, he said. More if they were lucky. He would teach the boys everything they would ever need to know to become men and the girl would grow up to be just like Shanta. She remembered how hysterically they laughed when they decided that if ever they had kids, they would use Muslim names like Ali or Safia. So neither family could lay claim.

It was a rainy afternoon in Bangalore when she realised she was pregnant. She spent the afternoon curled on the bed, waiting for him to come home, tears flowing into her ears, into a grey puddle on her pillow. He was ecstatic. He rubbed away her tears, saying that she had nothing to fear, she would make a great mother. But she knew that something was amiss. For months after, she could still feel the wetness in her ears, a reminder that something wasn't right.

A few weeks later he took her to a narrow lane near the Cantonment Railway Station and pointed to a new apartment building. "The third floor is ours," he whispered. "I just bought it. For you and me and the baby."

"Ma, can we buy an island?" interrupted Safia, from behind her green typewriter.

Shanta looked bewildered.

"What?"

"Can we buy an island? Just ... just like George and Timmy?"

"An island?"

"Like George and Timmy."

"Maybe, someday."

"Really, Ma?" Safia put down the dog-eared Enid Blyton that she had been reading for the past eighteen months. "Only for us? No outsiders allowed."

The following week, Shanta slipped in the bathroom and fractured her hip bone. Her days of recovery would be slow, predicted Dr Seshadri. Her bones had become brittle, he said, advising her to consult an osteoporosis specialist. Shanta scoffed at the idea. A little pain wouldn't trouble her, she wasn't made of chalk.

What would trouble her was Safia.

Shanta could clearly remember falling. She recalled the exhilarating fear as her body felled to the ground, free, as though possessed by wild youth. She remembered hearing the painful crack as the marble bathroom floor rose to her hip. She remembered her white cotton sari floating towards her in a slow dance.

Then she remembered hearing Safia before seeing Safia. Those clumsy overgrown footsteps thudding towards her. Then she saw Safia, standing over her, a big foolish smile plastered on her face.

"Help me," gasped Shanta, the rush of adrenaline leaving her white and helpless.

Safia started laughing, a slow chuckle that gradually eclipsed into hysteria. She began clapping her hands loudly.

"Call Mrs Krishnan, Safi." She tried to regain some authority in her voice.

"No!"

"Safi, please. I'm hurt."

"Ma, I want to have chicken. Chick-en."

"Safi."

"I want a leg bone. I want to suck on a leg bone." Safia pulled in her cheeks and started making sucking noises.

Shanta couldn't help but wonder if this was some kind of punishment, some kind of torment, of a disavowed God. The voice she had been throttling for the past forty-five years spoke. Had she given birth to a monster?

The doctor, what was his name, Mukherjee, had warned them of all the complications, of the benefits of a Caesarean and what not. Jerome had disagreed. He thought it was the duty of a woman to give birth naturally. Of course, he never forbade her. He simply told her to do what she thought best. So it was her decision to give birth naturally. What a natural birth it was. Thirteen hours it took. Safia came out blue, a miracle child, God's own, she thought with joy. Her joy was to be short-lived. Dr Mukherjee told her the strangled truth, foetal asphyxia.

Dr Mukherjee said she could have no more, her insides couldn't take it. There had been too much damage. She imagined Safia scratching and clawing her way out. There would be no boys for Jerome.

The year after Safia's birth, Jerome went to Germany, trading in cloth and aftershave. They would need the money, he said, now that they had Safia's medical expenses, therapy sessions, special schools to think of.

He always promised that things would get better. He would make it better. But in a few years his voice started sounding tired and without conviction. His face began to crease with anxiety, his salt-crusted skin aged like a drought plain. Shanta knew then that things would never go back.

Time twisted and turned, and so did Jerome. From Germany to Austria to Switzerland to Turkey. One country led to another, and over forty-five years, he was gone more than less. And then one morning, on March 31, 2007, she received a phone call to say that it was all over. He had died in Angola, unloved, unclaimed. She still didn't know whether to miss him or to curse him. He had left her alone, alone but for Safia.

The weeks and months after Shanta's injury, Safia became more and more tiresome. She refused to go to school with Ratna, who had slipped silently into the daily routine of things. And she refused to go alone.

"But why can't you go, Safia?"

"I can't, Ma." She was wailing into her towel.

"You've already missed so much school."

"I'll go only with you."

"Don't you miss school?"

"I do."

"You have to learn to manage by yourself."

"Why?"

"Because ... you just have to manage."

"I can't."

"What will Daddy say?"

"Daddy isn't here."

"No, he isn't."

A punctured orchestra of dogs began barking and howling from the parking lot.

"Bloody junglis," said Shanta, as she limped to the open balcony door. Ratna was standing there, peering at the ground.

"Don't see, Ajji."

"What is it?"

Ratna was cringing behind the pallu of her sari. "Nothing," she said quickly. "Just some strays fighting over a bone."

"I want to shoo them away."

"Don't come."

"Rubbish!"

Shanta felt a bitterness well up in her throat. A pack of dogs was tearing apart a lone stray, blood and bones ripping from his body as green faecal matter lay strewn around him.

"It is Moti," said Ratna.

"The lame one?"

"Yes."

They were both silent.

"Why, Ajji?" asked Ratna with a quiver in her voice .

"I don't know."

"It doesn't make sense."

"No, it doesn't."

"Someone should have protected him," said Ratna.

"Who?"

"Someone. God always places someone to protect those in need."

The dogs fell silent and a wave of calm pressed against Shanta.

The Transformation
Prashanti Talpankar

"Doctor Meena," someone called out from the hospital's reception counter.

"Good morning, Doctor Meena," someone else greeted her from another direction.

"Doctor Meena, Doctor Simon has called you to his office," a ward boy called out from a distance.

Meena responded cheerfully to the various greetings. People calling her a doctor gave her great pride. Her internship had recently ended and she had started work as a junior resident in the same medical college. So anyone calling her 'Doctor' tickled her with delight. She would clench her fist with a triumphant "Yesss!" This kind of a 'Yes!' has become a mannerism with young people nowadays, so what if twenty-three-year-old Dr Meena expresses herself this way!

But even at this young age, dreams of doing social work as a doctor shone in her eyes. That's how she had been brought up at home.

"Doctor Meenabai," yet another called out. The sound of briskly tapping heels brought Sister Isabel trotting up to her.

The Transformation

Sensing the urgency in Sister Isabel's pace, she asked her, "What is the matter, Sister?"

"Doctor, yesterday you had asked for that *ghantti* girl's report. Here, here's the report," the nurse said, handing her a file of papers.

Sister Isabel was one of the finest nurses at the hospital. Compassionate and noble, she truly upheld human values. Meena liked her very much. But at this moment she scowled at the nurse. This Goan habit of calling migrants by the derogatory term 'ghantti' always angered her. But her irritation was overcome by anxiety about the report in the nurse's hands. She decided to take up this name calling issue later with Isabel.

She took the report file from the nurse. "Anything serious, Sister?"

"Yes, Doctor, it's malaria—falciparum."

"What! Rashida has falciparum? Oh Lord! Sister, have you put her on medication?" a dismayed Meena asked Isabel.

"Yes, Doctor," said Isabel. Meena heaved a sigh of relief.

"I had given pills for all the malaria patients, Doctor. But it's better to bring this girl to the hospital, isn't it?" Meena nodded in agreement.

"So should I call an ambulance?"

"No, Sister, first we will have to locate this girl. It's difficult to find these migrant children in one place. When did you send her blood for testing?"

"Three days back. But her report came in today," replied Isabel.

Sheesh! This was the way these government hospitals worked! A report takes three days! But what could Meena do? This age old lethargy was not going to be overcome by one Meena.

She walked briskly, report in hand, to her scooter. She made some quick calculations. How long would it take to reach from here to the fish market? Twenty minutes? No problem. Anyway she was headed home, having finished her duty. This little detour would save a life.

Before she did this, she tried to phone Tara and Rehana. Both their phones were switched off. She looked at her watch. It was two. They must be teaching the kids at school. Better to go there first, she thought.

Tara and Rehana were roughly of her age. They had taken up this unconventional vocation of teaching at an informal school for street children.

This school was different from the others. It ran from one-thirty to three-thirty in the afternoon, for just two hours. It was named 'Itkuli Bitkuli Shalla'.

At about one-thirty, these hungry children would come running to the school. They would then wash their hands and feet and sit to eat what Tara and Rehana had brought for them—chapatis, bhaji, idlis, dosas and more. After eating, they would say a short prayer, followed by an hour of study—a fun kind of study—comprising playing carrom, cards, snakes and ladders, and singing songs. Through this they were taught maths, language and science. At three-thirty the children would disperse to their places of work.

They worked at the fish market, selling plastic bags and hawking lemons, vegetable and fish. Some of them would pack grocery items in shops. Each child's trade left its strong smell on him or her—the stench of fish, a coarse saltiness or of rotting fish entrails. Anyone standing in their midst would have flinched in disgust. But Rehana and Tara had grown accustomed to them.

The Transformation

Sometime in the past, Rehana had brought some children to the hospital for a check-up. She got to know Meena there. Their acquaintance grew into friendship and after some days Meena joined in helping Tara and Rehana at the school.

It was here that Meena had met Rashida. She was different from the rest of the children, with glowing skin and twinkling eyes. Her reddish brown hair was all tousled in curls. Her hair had never experienced coconut oil or the touch of a comb. She was quite smart and she loved studying.

Engrossed in her thoughts, Meena did not realise that she had already reached the school, close to the fish market. To her surprise, the school was shut. What had happened? Thousands of questions flashed through Meena's mind. No! Refusing to entertain negative thoughts, she tried dialling Tara and Rehana again. But she could not connect to them.

What was she to do now? Did something happen to Rashida? Did her fever rise? Were Tara and Rehana attending to her? The school students were also nowhere to be seen.

Meena walked from the school to the fish market. The stink and the squelchy ground of the place had always disgusted her. But that did not concern her today. Her eyes kept searching for the children's familiar faces.

Just then the children themselves spotted her. A group of them came running.

"Doctor, teacher, doctor, teacher, do you want a bag?" one of them offered her.

"Don't take his, teacher, take mine," called out another.

"Take mine, teacher, take mine," called out a third child.

All of them were known to her. But she couldn't recall their names. She would always mix them up. She would call

Rehman Amar, Amar would become Jitu, and she couldn't distinguish between Shannu and Dilawar.

But she knew some children very well. She spotted Resha and Wasim among them.

"Resha, where is Rashida?" Meena asked her.

"She hasn't come to the market, teacher," the child replied.

"She must be at home," volunteered Gangi, another familiar face.

"Where does she live?" Meena asked Gangi.

"She used to live in Chimbel, teacher. I don't know where she lives now," said Gangi and ran off to sell her plastic bags. The other children also moved off. Only Resha remained behind with Meena.

"What happened, dear?" a fisherwoman asked Meena. She may have recognised her as a teacher at the school. These fisherwomen and the street children had a strange bond. The former would usually yell at the latter and chase them off, but they would also help them in times of need.

"Aunty, have you seen that Rashida, with the reddish brown hair?" Meena asked her.

"Rashida? That Lamani girl or the one from Chimbel?" asked the fisherwoman. "Why are you looking for her? What has happened?"

"Rashida has malaria. See, her report has just come in. She needs to be admitted to the hospital," Meena told her.

"Rashida? I'm not sure. Check out near the riverside, there's a lot of shellfish being collected there. Poor girl!" The fisherwoman clucked in sympathy, but her pity was not for Rashida. She felt sorry for Meena, running after the poor children despite being a doctor.

Meena started her scooter. Four to five kids came running. "Teacher, teacher, I'm coming." "I'll show you the way!" They clamoured around her for a scooter ride.

"You are all coming? Then let's walk." At that they all went back to selling their bags, leaving only Resha and Nagi with the doctor.

The three of them went down by the riverside. It was low tide. They reached the spot where people were collecting basketfuls of shellfish from the river bed. But there was no auburn-haired Rashida. Meena called out "Rashida! Rashida!" Two Rashidas looked at her with wide eyes, like frightened rabbits. What was she to do now?

Just then Wasim came running to them. "Teacher, teacher, is it that Rashida with the black dress? She is in the garden, sitting on the swing," he said, panting for breath.

The garden was close by. From afar, Meena could see a girl on the swing. Sheesh! The resistance of these kids was incredible. Anyone else would have collapsed by now. And this girl was playing!

But was this really Rashida? Meena could only see her back. No, it was Rashida. She wore the same polka dotted black frock she had worn in the past. She had become really thin. The frock hung loose on her.

"Rashida, Rashida!" Meena called out to her.

"Rashida, she has come to take you," added Wasim.

The girl brought the swing to a halt and hopped off. And without looking backwards, she ran towards the huts behind the garden. Meena ran after her, calling out her name. Wasim caught up with the girl and grabbed her by her hair.

"Rashida, what nonsense is this! Don't you know me?" Meena turned the girl around to face her. But it wasn't Rashida. She did look like her, but she was not the girl they were looking for.

"Teacher, this is not Rashida," said Wasim as if he had made a significant discovery. "This is Rashida's sister."

"Where is Rashida?" Meena asked the girl gently. She seemed to be scared at being caught tightly by her hand. Wasim and Resha also kept asking her, "Where is Rashida, where has she gone?" For a long while the girl kept mum with her head bowed.

"Child, why are you so scared?" Meena asked her reassuringly. But again, she neither replied nor raised her head.

As if changing the topic, Meena asked, "Tell me, what is your name?"

"Najma," she replied.

"Najma, isn't this dress Rashida's?" Resha asked her.

The child nodded and began to cry. Meena was alarmed. Did something bad happen to Rashida? Why was Najma behaving like this? She remembered Tara and Rehana again, but then recalled Resha saying that they had gone out of Goa for a 'coniference'. Those two would have known what to do in a matter like this.

"Come Najma, show me your house," cajoled Meena, but Najma did not budge from the spot. Wasim and Resha too tried, but to no avail.

Meena glanced across at the huts. She saw a group of people gathered near one of the huts.

"Is that your house?" Meena gestured to Najma. She nodded. Meena broke into a sweat. Something bad had surely happened. She braced herself and walked toward the hut, followed by her two little foot soldiers.

Pools of stagnant water, heaps of garbage and the howl of stray dogs greeted her. She made her way through all this towards the gathered slum dwellers.

Amidst the huddle of people she saw a bearded man seated. In one hand he held a stick and in the other a peacock feather. A small girl sat in front of him and the crowd, fully naked except for a pair of panties. The bearded 'baba' was hitting her with the stick and then running the peacock feather over her head. The shivering girl was shrieking in pain.

Meena was filled with rage. What was this tamasha all about? She forgot all about Rashida. Only thinking of rescuing this child she fought her way through the crowd and confronted the quack. To her shock, the child was Rashida! Meena now seethed with anger. Rashida saw her and sobbed, "Teacher, teacher see, he is beating me!"

Meena snatched the stick away from the godman and shouted, "What is going on here? What are you doing?" All this happened in a flash. The bearded quack was taken aback for a moment, but quickly recovered.

"Hey, woman, step aside, move away. There's an evil spirit on this child. Someone has done black magic on her," he intoned, as he rolled his reddened eyes.

"Black magic nonsense! She has malaria. Look at this report! She has to be admitted to the hospital," Meena tried to explain.

"Let our children get fever or anything. We will take care of them," said a drunken man, probably Rashida's father.

"I am Doctor Meena from the government hospital. I have come to take her to the hospital," said Meena as she dialled the emergency number 108 on her cell phone.

"We will not send her to the hospital. Your tablets don't work on her. You have taken four days to come!" said Rashida's mother. Who would explain to her the difference between ordinary malaria and malaria falciparum? Meena was at a loss for words.

"Your pharmacies and hospitals are not for us poor people. They are only for rich people like you. Our local cures and our godman will make us alright," said another know-it-all. Rashida snuggled up to Meena.

Meena assessed the crowd. They were all staring at her as though she was a performing monkey.

"You may be a doctor or anybody, I will not let you take my daughter," Rashida's father stood in front of Meena like a coconut tree. He was also swaying like a coconut tree.

Meena did not reply. She gave him a cool look and asked Rashida, "Are you ready to go to the hospital, dear?"

"Yes, teacher," replied Rashida in a weak voice. She could barely stand up. Meena made her sit on the ground.

"Rashida, you will not go anywhere," commanded her father.

"Beti, come here, come to Ammi," her mother beckoned. Rashida clung to Meena even more tightly.

Meena thought, they are so many and I am alone ... no, no, Wasim and Resha are with me ... four of us against the rest of them. Even if the ambulance arrived, it would be tough to take Rashida away from here. The normally shy and scared Meena now became fearless. She dialled 100.

"Hello, Police Control Room? This is Doctor Meena, from the government hospital ... yes, I am at the hutments near the garden ... I need help to take a patient to the hospital... yes, I am waiting ..."

She dialled another number. "Hello, may I speak to DSP D'Souza? Uncle, Doctor Meena here ... I have asked the Control Room to help me with a patient, please request them to hurry ... Thank you, Uncle." Her father's close acquaintance was glad to help.

She looked around at everyone triumphantly. The crowd had now thinned out in fear. In a few moments they melted away like thawing ice. Only the four of them and Rashida's parents remained.

Meena picked up her phone again. "Hello, Doctor Meena here. Yes, Sister, I will be there in ten minutes with a patient. Yes, yes, Rashida. Keep a bed ready ... Thank you, Sister."

And another number. "Hello Operator, this is Doctor Meena, please connect me to the pathology lab ..."

Just this morning she had been tickled at being called 'Doctor'. And now she was eagerly and authoritatively working as a doctor. Her role playing days were over. This was the real thing. She was now truly Doctor Meena.

Originally written in Konkani as 'Rupantar'. Translated by José Lourenço .

The Return
Belinda Viegas

"Good morning, Rosa. You slept well? You want some tea?"

"No, I want coffee," says Rosa, slumping into a chair. "You don't have coffee?"

Milagrina looks up at her. "You ever drank coffee here? You know very well we don't have coffee here."

"Okay, okay. Give me tea. What else to do?" Rosa looks around and sees Celestine and Sebastian watching television. "Hello darlings. Come and give Mummy a kiss."

"They haven't gone to school today," says Milagrina. The children peck their mother on her cheek and hurry back to the film they are watching.

"Why you haven't gone to school?" Rosa asks.

"We wanted to be with you today," replies Celestine.

"How sweet! Come, give Mummy another kiss."

"They can still reach school in time," says Milagrina.

"Yes, yes. You must go to school and study big. So that you can become great officers."

"The way they are studying, they will only become peons in an office," says Milagrina.

"Why you are talking like this about my children? They will become great people in life."

"Great people, if they watch TV instead of going to school?"

"Yes, yes, children. Milagrin-aunty is right. Put off the TV and get ready for school."

"No, no, Mummy. See, this new film is going on. Please, Mummy. Only today. After all, it is the first day you have come home."

"Rosa, you want them to become clever, or what?"

"Yes, Milagrina, yes. School is important. Celestine, Sebastian, you can watch TV when you finish school."

"No, Mummy. See what Hrithik Roshan is doing now! He is so handsome. See how he is dancing."

"No, Celestine. Put off the TV and go to school."

Celestine continues watching the film.

"Sebastian! Put off the TV and go to school!"

Sebastian does not respond.

"Milagrina! Tell them to go to school!"

"Why should I tell them? *You* are their mother. *You* tell them!"

Rosa looks uncertainly at her children. She opens her mouth and closes it again without saying anything. Then she turns to Milagrina. "Let them be. It is anyway too late now. And after all, it *is* my first day at home. Let them be!"

"Let them be?" asks Milagrina sharply.

Rosa puts her elbows on the table and holds her head tiredly. "Where is my tea? I had such a terrible night. And

I thought I would have such a good sleep in my own bed after two years."

"Your own bed is too hard now?"

"Yes, I must get a new mattress."

"You already have a mattress. Not like us, still sleeping on mats on the hard floor."

"So now I should buy you all new beds and fancy mattresses?"

"I never said that."

"You are not happy with the two new rooms, the TV, the fridge and the washing machine?"

"I never said I wasn't."

Milagrina places a cup of tea in front of Rosa. Rosa takes a sip.

"I need more sugar."

Milagrina plonks the bottle of sugar with a thump on the table. "Now the tea is not sweet enough?"

"Who is paying for the sugar, Milagrina? Can I not have as much as I want?"

"Anytime I say you cannot?"

Rosa adds another teaspoon of sugar into her cup and stirs her tea. Then she takes a loud sip. "I can't drink this tea!" she says, pushing the cup away. "I need to have coffee."

"We don't have any coffee."

"Then we must buy some."

"Who will go to the shop? I have so much work to do."

"I will ask Sebastian. Sebastian!"

There is no response.

"Sebastian!"

"Yes, Mummy?" Sebastian is clearly annoyed.

"Sebastian, darling, I need some coffee. You are a good boy. Go to the shop and buy me some."

"Not now, Mummy. I will go later, as soon as the film is over."

"Sebastian, I'm telling you I want the coffee now, not later! Otherwise I will get a headache."

"Tell Celestine to go."

"Why me? Mummy asked you first. So why should I go?"

"Why should *I* go?" Sebastian continues sitting and watching.

Rosa gets up, walks over to the telly and switches it off. "Okay. This is better?"

Sebastian turns the television set on again. "Don't be angry, Mummy. We are so happy you have come back."

"But I want my coffee."

"I will buy some as soon as the film is over. I promise."

Rosa sighs. "Okay." She returns to the table, where Milagrina is shelling peas.

"Milagrina, what are you cooking? I have such a longing for pork. That is the one thing I miss so much in Saudi Arabia."

"I thought you got *everything* in Saudi."

"Not pig's flesh. Can you make vindaloo today? And sannas also?"

"Why? You have forgotten how to cook?"

"Milagrina! You know I am on holiday now. You know how hard I have to work there? Cleaning and swabbing. Everything must be shiny-finey. Not like this." Rosa draws a finger on the back of the chair next to her and looks at the dirt on it.

Milagrina throws the last of the peas down into the bowl and glares at Rosa. "You think I sit here on my bum the whole day long and do nothing? Who has to look after the house? And run after *your* children?"

"My children are good children."

"Oh, yes? Look at your daughter. She only wants to watch TV and make eshtyle. And Sebastian. I will not be surprised if he is smoking and drinking with his friends."

"And what you are doing? You are allowing that? Why did I leave them in your care? To let them do whatever they want?"

"Did you teach them to listen? They don't know how to listen!"

"What you mean, Milagrina? They are good children!"

"Good children? Listen to their teachers. Only complaints, complaints, complaints!"

"What complaints?"

"They are zero in lessons."

"But I am sending money for tuitions. You are not sending them for tuitions?"

"Of course I am sending them. But the tuition teacher is also complaining. They are not learning and are also disturbing the other children."

"Then what you are doing?"

"What I can do? They are not listening."

"What do you mean they are not listening? You have to make them listen!"

"How? Did you teach them how to listen?"

"They are good children!"

"So the problem is with me, or what?"

"I never said that." Rosa turns to the children. "Celestine! Sebastian! Milagrin-aunty tells me you are not studying properly. Don't make stupid faces, Sebastian! How you will become a big man?"

"Mummy, the teacher is against me. How can I study if she is always shouting at me?"

Rosa turns to Milagrina. "How can he study if the teacher is always shouting at him?"

Milagrina points a carrot at Celestine. "What about her?"

Rosa looks at Celestine who is totally engrossed in the film. "Celestine! Why you are not learning?"

"Lessons are so boring," Celestine replies without taking her eyes from the screen.

"Everything is so boring for them," says Milagrina. "Ask her if she ever lifts a finger to help to do any work here?"

"Why should she?"

Milagrina stands up and looks at Rosa. "So I have to do everything here? Like a servant?"

"I am sending you the money, no?"

"You think I am working like a dog because of your money? I am only doing all this because they are my brother's children. Not because of your money!"

"If your brother was not a drunkard, I would have to leave my children and go so far away to work so hard?"

"To work so hard? You are always only telling how great your life there is."

"Yes. There I have everything so posh. Here, what is there?" Rosa bangs the cup of tea on the table. "Not even coffee."

"Then why you came back? Only to make me work for you also?"

"I never said that, Milagrina. Why you think like that?"

"Mummy, Mummy," Celestine calls, pointing excitedly to the television set. "Look! We also must get Tata Sky!"

Rosa looks at the advertisement going on. "Tata Sky? But I already paid for the cable connection."

"That is not good, Mummy. Tata Sky is much, much better. Please Mummy. Please say yes! It will make me so happy!"

Rosa gets up and goes over to her daughter. She pinches her cheek gently and kisses her fingers with a loud smack. "Of course, my darling. Anything to make you happy."

"Mummy, don't forget. Last time when you went to Saudi, you promised to buy me a new bike," puts in Sebastian.

"He's only sixteen years old," says Milagrina.

Sebastian gets up agitatedly. "But Mummy, you promised! You promised!"

"You promise you will study and listen to Milagrin-aunty?" asks his mother fondly.

"Yes, yes! You know which type bike I want? A yellow Hero Honda Karizma!"

"You promise you will study nicely and become a great man?"

"Yes, Mummy! Yes!" Sebastian jumps up pumping his arms in the air in a victory gesture. "Thank you. I love you, Mummy!"

"I love you too, Mummy," says Celestine.

"I must go tell my friends about my new bike," says Sebastian as he walks towards the door.

"And I must tell my friends about our new Tata Sky," says his sister following him out of the door.

"See how happy I made them," says Rosa smiling happily.

Neruda in November

Marilia Priyanka Fernandes

It was a crisp November morning. The cool air rushed up her nostrils and collected in her lungs. Nothing could beat the beauty of November in Assagao. It had always been her favourite month. Everything sparkled in the brilliance of the morning sun. Its warmth seeped into one's very being, driving away any sadness. The birds revelled in their orchestra and the butterflies in the garden danced to their merry melodies.

She stepped out of her ancestral villa and inhaled deeply again. A smile spread over her face as she clutched the book of poems closer to her. They were waiting for her. Beckoning her in their frills of orange. Freshly anointed with morning dew. Slender in the dancing breeze.

"Good morning my beauties," she said with adoring warmth.

"It's Neruda once again," she spoke very matter-of-factly, the sparkle in her eye betraying the passionate love she had for the Chilean's poetry.

She opened a page:

*"Before I loved you, love, nothing was my own:
I wavered through the streets, among
Objects:
Nothing mattered or had a name:
The world was made of air, which waited.*

*I knew rooms full of ashes,
Tunnels where the moon lived,
Rough warehouses that growled 'get lost',
Questions that insisted in the sand ..."*

"Ooooooo Laura!!!......" The shrill voice of her neighbour, Antonette, pierced the poem.

"Talking to yourself again, eh? When will you stop this morning madness? It's been nine years now. He's gone. You have to move on. What is the point of talking to these abolim? They don't understand you. It makes you look cuckoo."

Laura gave her a mild smile, as if to say no one could ever understand.

"Just the other day Josephine was aksing me whether you are mental."

"It's asking, Antonette, not aksing," Laura said, a bit irritated, hoping this would drive away her nosy but well meaning neighbour.

It worked.

Miffed about being corrected, Antonette hurried off for the seven o'clock Mass.

Laura picked up the sprinkler and began her morning ritual of watering the abolim.

It was mid-November, and these flowers which appear usually in January had already bloomed in her garden. Why she loved the abolim so much she didn't know. Maybe it was their bright orange energy. Or that they were delicate, fragile and demanded a tender touch. Or was it because they never received the attention a rose or marigold got? The reason was a mystery to her.

She thought about what Antonette had just said. She did not expect her or anyone else to understand. It had been love at first sight—the day she read her first novel by Jane Austen. Dickens, Saki, Stevenson, the Bronte sisters and Chekov followed in quick succession. She would blissfully lose herself in their world for hours. Much to her mother's dismay, her father let her complete her Masters in English Literature. But on one condition: she would have to marry as soon as she got her degree. She agreed and went off to university.

It was during her years at university that she had first chanced upon Pablo Neruda. The sensuality of his poetry enchanted her. She wondered at the depth of this man's emotions. His blatant expressions and bizarre analogies held her captive. His poetry was her opium. She was a prisoner of his words. Yet she found freedom in his fluid language. Unlike Keats and Johnson with their measured meter and rhyme, Neruda was wild and uncontained. He appealed to her sensual spirit and she responded with unabashed adulation.

Two years had flown faster than a kite chasing a robin. Her mother was the first to remind her of her part of the deal. She wondered why mothers were so eager to snatch a daughter's freedom. The whole family got into gear, hunting for a suitable match. He had to be Goan, Catholic and, of course, a Brahmin. Education, modernism, even Catholicism could not uproot the centuries-old roots of caste from their hearts. They were carefully replanted and nurtured, generation after generation.

Laura watched the proceedings with amusement, dread and anticipation. Many of her school friends were already married. She had heard mixed stories. None of the young, educated men she met had ever heard of Neruda. Her mother almost had a heart attack when she learned the poet was the cause of the rejected proposals. She blamed her husband for Laura's unthinkable, ridiculous demands.

"How can she reject doctors, lawyers and engineers for some stupid poet? That too he lives in her head! What face will I have now?" she screamed at him.

That's when Lawrence Abreu entered her life. Tall, and according to her mother handsome, he seemed like the perfect match for fragile Laura.

"Even their names sound good together. Like a match made in heaven!" cooed her mother while throwing dagger looks at Laura.

This time Laura did not talk about Neruda. Lawrence was happy to have a well educated wife. Not that she would ever have to use her education. He had a flourishing practice as a lawyer in Mapusa.

Their marriage was a grand affair, he being the only son, and she the only daughter. And that is how Laura Cordeiro from Saligao, now Laura Abreu, came to live in the village of flowers—Assagao.

Her in-laws had adored her. But then she never gave them reason to do otherwise. The days assumed an insipid routine after their short honeymoon in Calangute. She had once tried to read Neruda to Lawrence. He had just smiled and patted her head as if she were an amusing child. Lawyers have no need for poetry.

One day, three months after their honeymoon, Lawrence had returned home with a bunch of red roses. But their lovemaking had turned dry, like reading one of his boring briefs. She felt relieved when it ended. She had thought that maybe if she dressed up he would notice her, desire her. So she wore a pretty dress and did up her hair and face. But once again she felt like a plain white paper on which he hammered his cases in boring black ink. After this her spirit settled into a burning ember. Reading Neruda was painful. It only reminded her of what she could never dream of having. It would be easier for her if she smothered her spirit.

But only if she knew ... One can't totally annihilate the essence of a being forever. It lives somewhere deep inside like a dormant seed.

Then, suddenly, thirty-one years after marriage, at the age of sixty, her husband had a massive heart attack and slipped into the night. Laura's regular routine was disrupted. She missed him like one misses the chimes of a grandfather clock. Now she was left all alone in their villa. She had tried living in Australia where her children had migrated. But the place hadn't agreed with her. So she returned after a year. That's when she rediscovered the treasure of books she had buried in the attic. And now, despite herself, the dormant seed had begun germinating.

The garden was turning into an inferno as the sun rose higher. Laura picked up her book and retreated into the house.

Early next morning while she was once again in the garden, a taxi arrived next door. Laura caught a glimpse of the passenger. He was tall and lanky, like the electricity pole in the corner. She had heard he was coming from London. But she had felt that most people who came from there were more like the fat church bell. He had a number of large boxes which took a while to unload. The car obstructed her view, so she got back to her flowers and her poetry.

At eleven o'clock she heard a soft knock on her front door. "Who is it?" she asked.

"Rakesh," replied a soft, deep voice from the other side of the door.

He stood there with a parcel in his hands. It was his eyes—striking, intense and brown—that transfixed her. He could have melted anyone with his long stare. His greying hair contrasted with his young face. It fell straight over his eyes like a school boy. Laura couldn't guess his age. He could have been thirty or sixty. This enigma made her stare at him longer.

"I'm your new neighbour, Rakesh Kamat," he said, extending his right hand.

"I'm Laura. Do come in."

"Laura," he repeated her name. She liked the way he stressed the first syllable.

"So you have come from London. Which part of London did you live in?"

"Sheffield. I bought this house from Mrs Frias. The moment I saw this place I knew it had to be mine. The rolling hills and green valleys just draw you into their embrace. And each season is refreshingly invigorating. This land just welcomes you and claims you for its own."

Laura revelled in the words he used to describe her village.

"Even our people here are as varied as the landscape. Each one has a different story to tell. What better inspiration could I ask for? And besides, London is not home. Especially when you are used to warm climates and warm people, right?"

"So you're a writer then?" she asked with great enthusiasm.

Her eager response made him smile. Like the rising sun, it started at the centre of his mouth and spread to cover his entire face before he could say yes.

"What do you write? Novels, stories or boring text books?" she demanded. It's very easy for anyone to call himself a writer these days, she thought.

"Mostly novels and an occasional short story." His eye caught the book of poems lying on the table.

"You like poetry?" he queried.

"I love it passionately. My favourite is Neruda," she said with a broad smile.

"Don't you find him irrelevant at times?" he challenged her.

"Only for those who lack the seventh sense—aesthetics," she shot back, eyes blazing.

He laughed softly. "I agree."

"Do you write poetry?"

"Only when I have the perfect muse," he replied looking straight at her, and Laura blushed.

"Poetry is not easy," he continued. "It puts you in a trance. You sometimes have to lose a bit of your sanity to express the profound."

Laura admired his ability to express his feelings and thoughts in precise words.

The sound of a gate opening distracted them. Old houses in Goa don't need a bell. Each gate whistles a different pitch, heralding the arrival of a visitor. It was José, the caretaker. He had come to inquire about the new owner. Rakesh left for his house. Laura watched him as he walked down the steps. Deep down she knew that their paths would cross again.

It's ridiculous, thought Laura. Is it normal for a woman my age to be attracted to a man? Despite her rationalisations she couldn't stop thinking of this morning's conversation with Rakesh. She thought about his ability to say things so beautifully, and his captivating brown eyes. Something about him made her feel very comfortable. Like sitting in one's favourite armchair. The harder she tried to suppress the thought of him, the more he entered her mind.

The abolim were dancing in the light November breeze. The wind caressed their petals and rushed through their leaves. The cacophony of roosting birds announced the arrival of dusk. Everything was bathed in a warm orange light. A slight chill was spreading as the sun retreated and made way for the moon. Laura sat in her garden reading aloud.

"Neruda," she heard a soft voice whisper. He had entered her garden silently and now stood behind her.

"Allow me the liberty of saying this," he said as he dropped to the grass beside her. "You look beautiful in the evening light."

Her eyes glistened in the dusk. No one had ever said these words to her so sincerely. She longed for him to touch her.

He took the book from her hands and began reading. Everything around seemed to be lulled by his soft, calming baritone as he read Neruda.

"I do not love you as if you were salt-rose, or topaz,
or the arrow of carnations the fire shoots off.
I love you as certain dark things are to be loved,
in secret, between the shadow and the soul.

I love you as the plant that never blooms

but carries in itself the light of hidden flowers;
thanks to your love a certain solid fragrance,
risen from the earth, lives darkly in my body..."

Time has a strange quality. Sometimes all it takes is one moment, one experience ... And this single moment can overshadow an eternity.

The sun had set. A strange warmth filled Laura's heart and spilled over till it percolated into her bones. She had never felt this connected to another human being. She moved closer to him. His intense eyes looked into hers.

Somewhere the shadows moved, and Antonette's head bobbed over the fence, the juice of fresh gossip still dripping from her lips. But she just stood there, her mouth open, gaping like a foolish fish caught on a hook.

He read poetry the way it should be read, giving life to the words.

"I love you without knowing how, or when, or from where.
I love you straightforwardly, without complexities or pride;
so I love you because I know no other way

than this: where I does not exist, nor you,
so close that your hand on my chest is my hand,
so close that your eyes close as I fall asleep."

Paradise of Fools
Ramnath Gawde

As Vasu sat waiting for the stark heat of the afternoon sun to subside, his heart fluttered uneasily. The bidi in his fingers kept entering and leaving his lips ceaselessly, as though wanting to extinguish itself quickly. One couldn't really tell whether the smoke from that bidi was entering his belly or filling his heart or just dissipating into the air. Of late he had fallen victim to the habit of hungrily devouring and spewing smoke, like some fireplace. Usually he was a tiger at work, if he set his hand to some job he would not rest until he had accomplished it. But though physically still fit, age was closing in on Vasu.

He turned to look at his own shadow. Then shaking himself out of his reverie he quickly rose to his feet. He picked up the pan and hoe at his side and without caring for the noon heat began walking briskly forward. But the shouts from his grandson trotting behind compelled him to turn around. He knew the little fellow would not rest until his grandfather lifted him up. He hoisted the boy onto his shoulders and even as his daughter-in-law called out not to take him, he continued walking.

These days he was digging a well nearby. Labourers and women helpers were not easy to come by. If they turned up for two days, they would abscond for four days. So without waiting for the workers, he had gotten to work, his old bones hammering away at the rocky ground and getting his guts into a real twist. That well had become a great test of his own existence.

He placed his grandson in the shade of a cashew tree and after tying a towel to his head he began to cut away at the rock. Within instants the body that had been yearning for water for so long broke out into rivulets of sweat. The grandfather was digging, then how could the grandson stay quiet? He too picked up a small stick and a coconut shell and began to scoop out his own well on the pile of excavated soil. His tiny four year old frame was baking in the heat, his little hands and legs getting scorched. But his anxiety was no lesser than his grandfather's, and soon trickles of sweat ran down his skin too. From his running nose ran little streams of snot caked with thick red dust.

Watching the efforts of his grandchild, Vasu's cheeks flushed with pride. "*Arrey* babu, don't come this side, *anhh*, you may fall. Play there only, on your side. Until the workers come, I will dig only this much. Then I will break some tender cashew nuts and give you. Get along, go play in that shade, okay!"

But was his grandson one to listen? He was deeply engrossed in building his well. As it shaped up, sweat kept pouring down his fired up little body.

Vasu who had opened his mouth, would not stop. Whether he was chatting with his grandson or just unburdening himself wasn't very clear. "That miner has become greedy and is now out to finish us. How well that spring was flowing. When we dammed up the stream, our fields would get enough water all through the summer. I didn't raise such a large plantation just like that. I broke the rocks and grew coconut saplings there. Alongside the bandh I grew banana trees. I cultivated bhaji and greens and fed so many people. In the month of May when all other wells would dry up, people would come from all over to this spring, to bathe and drink water. And now, even before the Sounsvar Padvo ... we are struggling for a drop of water. God, what will become of us in the future! Where are we to get water for our fields and orchards and for our cattle! The new coconut and arecanut saplings had nicely taken root. How will their lives be saved now? Lord God, I am tired of calling out to you. I laid my faith in you and took up my hoe. I sharpened my pickaxe. Now you will just have to take this urge of mine and bring it to fruition ..."

He paused and vigorously spat on his hands, and after rubbing them together gripped the handle of the pickaxe again.

His grandson was watching him with narrowed eyes. He couldn't understand what his grandfather was saying, and to whom. Other than himself, there was no one else around. Then why was grandfather muttering away? He had felt like asking him a couple of times. But seeing the old man lost in his own world, the boy kept quiet.

By this time two women helpers had turned up and they hailed Vasu—"Dado, what stories are you telling your grandson?"

But he didn't feel like replying to them. He glanced towards the sun to estimate the time and then picking up the pans he began to fill them himself, with a listless air.

After they were filled he rested a hand on his hip and waited for the helpers. But for a long while they showed no sign of descending the steps of the excavated well. Their preparation for work seemed to be never ending. Vasu's voice rose—"Hey, aren't you two done? Have you seen where the day has reached? And where has that Raghu gone? I can't dig anymore."

"Ask his son! Babu, where has your Papa gone? To gamble at matka or gone fishing?"

"When will this son of mine get some sense! He has become a husband and a father and still he craps around. He can't take care of what he has inherited. How will he grow and eat anything, God only knows!"

"Dado, somebody seems to be measuring some land down there."

"Measuring land? Oh, the panchayat said they are going to build a small bandh across the stream."

"If they are building a bandh then why are they measuring the cashew slopes?"

"They must be estimating how far the water will reach."

"If they were of the panchayat, wouldn't at least one of them have been known to us?"

"Then who are they?"

"Who knows! They were glaring at us for looking at them. They fixed some kind of glass machine on a stand and were taking photographs."

Now Vasu could not wait any longer. His mind began throbbing with anxiety. As though someone had pulled him up, he climbed the well's steps and after instructing the workers, he moved away quickly. The effort of digging the well had not tired him much but now he laboured to stride forward. Because he knew his fears had now taken the shape of a real demon and were coming true.

The mining pit in the distance was slowly turning into a fearsome sight. As it went deeper, it kept widening rapidly. As it consumed the hills one by one, it swallowed up numerous meadows and spaces. Now the tentacles of the mine were slowly crouching towards the adjacent lands. Just as a demoness confuses the minds of her victims and then swallows them up, so too these mines first choke the villages with dust and then devour all the water, the forests, the fields and orchards one by one. Along with humans, cats and mice and countless other creatures of nature are just played with. And now Vasu was running along like a mouse chased by a fiend. His destination was nearby, but he felt he was not walking quickly enough. He wanted to get there before they finished their measuring, as if whatever land they measured would be acquired by them.

"Hey, what are you doing there!" Vasu yelled as soon as he saw them. The lad who was marking the measurements with a red staff quickly moved off, as though fearful of being assaulted, and sat in a jeep that was parked nearby.

"With whose permission have you come here, anhh? Taking measurements as though it is your father's property! Get out immediately, I have already told your owners and sahebs whatever I have to say. There's no need for you to come here and set fire to our houses and homes ... " He kept shouting whatever came to his lips, seething in anger. He was exhausted with that frantic walking, but his tongue was raging away.

No one spoke up. He was panting now and he paused for a while. Then a surly man from the jeep spoke up— "Vasudad, come here. Just because we have surveyed your land does it mean that you *have* to give it to us? You give it if you want, otherwise ... "

"Arre, despite my having said 'no' a thousand times, how dare you step here!"

"You are right. But look, we have bought that land next to yours and to locate its boundaries we have to do this surveying."

"I have already shown your manager the entire plan and warned him that if he deviates anywhere he better watch out. Then how did you turn up here?"

"So your son hasn't told you anything?"

"Damn him," cursed Vasu. That son had ruined everything. Despite telling him not to, he had given that man copies of all their plans and documents.

"Alright, forget it. Now what do you want me to do?" asked the surveyor. "If you tell me to go, I will go." And before Vasu could say anything further, he started up his jeep and drove away down the stony road.

Feeling faint with hunger and thirst Vasu dragged himself onto a dried fallen trunk and sat pressing his forehead in the scorching heat.

Over the next few days a lot of cars and jeeps were to be seen coming to Vasu's land. But one day on seeing a police jeep at his door, Vasu's heart sank in dismay. Usually on seeing anyone's vehicle, his mouth would promptly open. But on seeing the khaki uniforms he fell quiet.

"Yes, Saheb, what did you want?" His son stepped forward with a smile, as though he knew one of them.

"The Inspector has asked both of you to come to the police station at ten o'clock."

"Called us? What is the matter, Saheb?"

"You will know when you come there."

"Is there any problem?" asked Vasu.

"There's a complaint against you for building an illegal compound wall."

"Then this must be the company's mischief. But that wall does not fall in their property. And that is not a recently built wall, it must be at least 25 to 30 years old. We only rebuilt it. Did they see it only now!"

"We don't know about that. If you have any documents or license, bring them along," the constable said and left. They were soon far way, but Vasu continued to look in their direction with a stunned look. Then he dumbly returned to his house and laid a hand on his hoe. But he felt he had no strength to lift it.

What happened the next day was not unexpected. His wall was declared illegal, the cowshed was illegal and they began to say that his cultivation was illegal too. On hearing this, the son quickly gave in. But Vasu silently resolved to fight it out to the end.

He was thus entangled in many lawsuits over the next few months and was severely harassed. He had to hire lawyers to defend his cases. His house stood alone at some distance from the village, yet he approached many villagers to warn them. But every one of them sought only their own selfish gains. As though money, cars and luxuries were their sole ambitions in life.

As the court cases mounted, new baits were being offered, but he did not yield to anyone. Then one morning, two cars turned up at his door. No one paid them any heed. After a while the occupants stepped out one by one and came to Vasu's courtyard.

Vasu was washing his mouth, making vigorous sounds. One couldn't make out whether he was coughing or scraping his tongue or whether he was spitting on someone. His visitors waited until his rituals were finished. Then one of them spoke up.

"Vasudad ..."

"Arrey, I have told you all a thousand times, I don't want to destroy my fields and get ruined. You will give me some money and I will survive for some four days. What are my children to do after that!"

"Why do you say so? You can buy property that is much better than this one, with the money that you will get. Besides we will give your son two trucks to start his business ..."

"No, no! I don't want anything of yours. We are happy as we are, by the grace of God."

"Alright, then at least tell us what you have to say."

"What I have to say? Have you fulfilled your promises all these years? You only make beggars out of our people. Is anybody happy? You bought all our Madhu's fields and lands. You placated him very well. But where are all his lakhs of rupees?"

"Our company had no dealing with Madhu. Those who have dealt with us now have plenty of trucks, cars, good houses and everything. Tomorrow your son too will move around in style. You will build a concrete house and buy a car."

On hearing this Raghu could not hide his excitement. But Vasu did not want to listen to any of their talk. "Don't show me those burnt dreams. Go and find some other fool." Saying this, he turned and stormed back towards his house.

"Look here, Vasudad, the company has increased its offer. They have decided to give five lakhs more and you will also get a car," the mining official urged him.

But after Vasu left, a curtain fell on that discussion and all the others also gradually went away.

As the summer warmth rose, these issues also began to get fired up.

The women began dancing the *dhalo* in the fields. The ripening rice stalks began to droop with the heat. The leaves of many plants wilted for lack of water. Seeing this, Vasu became restless. His ability to sleep had already long gone. One early morning he woke up from a dreadful dream, and began rousing everyone in the house to get to work on the excavation of the well. But seeing that no one else was ready to go, he hoisted his hoe onto his shoulder and set out. He laboured alone on the well and continued until he was tired. As he sensed that anytime now the spring would burst forth, he felt lightened. He saw that the workers and helpers would take some time to turn up and began to move around his fields.

Just then his daughter-in-law arrived with his tea and called out—"Dado, the police jeep has come. They have called you to the mines."

He kept quiet and after having his tea he got back to work.

After a while his son and his daughter-in-law reminded him—he had been summoned to the mines.

Still he ignored their calls. He eagerly wanted to see the spring burst forth in the well. The floor had already become wet and soggy.

As the sun rose in the sky, the pace of work slowed down.

The jeep that had visited in the morning returned. A police constable came directly to the well, spoke sternly to Vasu and then went away.

On hearing those menacing words Vasu felt a little apprehensive. He thought for a while and then, as was his habit, he slung the hoe onto his shoulder and started walking.

Paradise of Fools

On seeing him go towards the mines, his son got a bit worried. "Arrey baba, why are you taking that hoe?"

Vasu looked at his hoe and for a moment felt slightly odd. Yet he felt it was like a part of his own body and could not bring himself to put it down. He blurted—"On my way back I will get its edge sharpened."

Raghu did not fail to notice his father's pitiable condition. He too followed him. The burden of anxieties kept increasing on their heads like a load of stones.

When they reached the mining office, a number of cars were already parked there. Sensing that atmosphere, Vasu tensed up. Someone noticed him coming and took him directly to where the managers were seated.

Seeing the mood inside the office, Vasu was filled with dread. As he entered, the ongoing discussion abruptly stopped.

"Hey Vasudad, come, come and sit. And who are you roaming around to kill, with that hoe!" One of them laughed and gave him a chair. But Vasu did not sit. He kept his hoe at his feet and remained standing.

"So have you made your decision?" the other came straight to the point.

"What is there to decide? I don't want to give my land."

The moment he said this, everyone pounced on him.

"Your land! What is your land! That land belongs to the government. That whole area comes under the scope of our company. Will you see the plan?"

"I don't know about that. I pay a *foro* to the mamlatdar and I also pay tax to the panchayat."

"Still, the rights on the land belong to us. Do you want to see? Can you read? This is your son, right? Come here and see, and tell your father."

"What will he see! We don't want to see anything. My ancestors worked on those mountains and turned them into cultivable lands. Just because you say it is yours, how can it become yours?"

"That is why we are paying you money, isn't it? And tell me one thing, with whose permission are you digging that well? Do you have a license to dig there?"

"Why do I need a license? I am digging for water. Such a good stream used to flow there all through the year. Because of your mines everything dried up. The spring also vanished. Now to drink a sip of water, not even muck can be found."

"Spring? Stream? What are you talking about? There is nothing there."

"Then how did we cultivate so much crop on this land?"

"Okay, if you think we are lying, ask the Saheb here. He is a government officer. He will not lie."

"Vasu, they are telling the truth," said the officer. "Look here, this is the plan of the property you are talking about. Check it minutely. Here is your house and your field. But there is no spring or stream or well to be seen here."

"No no, Saheb, it has to be somewhere or the other."

"Why should I lie to you. See here, you can see it clearly. And even if there is any, it becomes government property. Not yours."

"And Vasu, look at this government approved Regional Plan. In this, all this land is shown under mining lease."

As they argued away Vasu felt he was being fired upon and torn apart from all four sides. He could not figure out whom to listen to and what to answer to whom. The huge multicoloured plan sprawled on that table seemed to be out to gobble him.

"Saheb, there must be some mistake in your plan. The plan that I have shows everything."

"We have a copy of your plan. There's nothing on that either."

"How is that possible? It must be there. How can anyone live without water?"

"We don't know about that. But on this plan other than your house there is nothing. Then how will the spring be there!"

"It will be there, it must be there, Saheb. My eyesight has gone bad. But surely you will be able to see it, Saheb. Raghu, you see, if you can locate our spring somewhere there!"

"What will he tell you! He can show you only if it is actually there!"

"No no, it must be there. Look here, it is definitely here. It is a mark of the goddess. How can it disappear?"

"My dear fellow, it is not there. See here, we have a number of plans, but other than the mines there are absolutely no springs or streams on any of these plans."

"No, it is there, it is there! It is exactly here. Arre, it is not just a spring, it is the goddess emerging from the heart of the mountain. How can it vanish? It is here, look, it is here!" he said tapping his finger persistently at a certain point on the plan.

But even then they denied its existence. Their adamant posturing and denials made Vasu's head spin and he felt giddy. He didn't know what was happening to him. He felt as though someone was pecking the life out of him, causing unbearable pain.

"Hey, don't simply bang your fingers here like that," barked the officer. "You won't find anything there."

"No, no, you will find! That spring did not come up just yesterday. It was a divine creation even before Man was born. Rivers and waters don't come into existence just like that! Look here, look here, it's right here!"

And he lifted his hoe like a man possessed and struck at the plan spread out on the table. He kept hitting it in a frenzy, again and again and again ...

Originally written in Konkani as 'Pisheak Peepal'. Translated by José Lourenço. 'Pisheak Peepal' shared the third prize at the Fundação Oriente Short Story Competition 2011.

The Homecoming

Cordelia Francis

As he locked the door to his workshop, Theodore Fernandes felt himself settle into a familiar calm and he knew all was well. In his carefully crafted world, things were kept simple and austere. He believed nothing in life was to be met with too much exuberance. So much so, the highs and lows that at times infiltrated his world were met with stoic reservation.

He was a religious man. Everyday he and his wife attended the first Mass at 6 o'clock at their parish church. While in other households TV had come to replace the murmurings of the Angelus, in Theodore's home the Hail Marys carried on year after year. It was as if time stood still at the Fernandes' threshold.

Everyone in the village gossiped about Theodore's unbending nature. Some humorously questioned whether the condition of his rigidity extended below the waist. Others pitied his wife Martha lamenting, "Poor thing, what she has to go through, living with a man like that!" Yet they never missed a ladinh. They knew Theodore was no miser. The cross would be whitewashed and decked with garlands of marigold, festooned with fairy lights and candles. After prayers, as the sun dipped, plum cake, samosas and patties were piled high on plastic trays and all ate to their heart's content. The men downed their thimbles of feni and the women delicately sipped their glasses of port wine.

Theodore had spent the past 58 years of his life chipping away at the frills and pleasures others spend their lives pursuing. Within himself he fought battles everyday believing that one day he would conquer all those emotional uprisings. Everyone, he believed, had a purpose in life and nothing should distract one from it. And so with single minded fervour he took on each of his acquired roles—as a husband, a strict father, a God-fearing man, a hardworking sailor who steadily rose to captain a merchant navy ship.

In retirement, Theodore felt he could relax a little, take a break from his strict routine. So he built a comfortable home in Aldona and gave himself to his true calling—sculpting. But even in his most creative flow, he absolved himself of carving anything other than Christian iconography.

He considered his natural flair for wood carving a God-given gift and hence with simple logic, Theodore devoted his skill to carving the somber faces and demure stances of Christian saints. Imagination was an indulgence and he was careful to keep it in check fearing it might lead him into carving images of idols. So when ordinary faces, limbs, even entire human dramas revealed themselves from their grainy textures of wood, he refused to be their liberator. Instead he superimposed these stirring images with replicas of Jesus, Mary, angels, saints and numerous crosses of varying sizes, copied from photographs, paintings and other statues. His replicas lined the niches of several churches which had either lost their artefacts to thieves or had them sidled off to antique dealers by their pastoral caretakers.

It was during the commission of a large cross that Theodore began to spend time with Father Pinto. A rotund man who was given to sagging, bulging and sponginess. One time, Father Pinto remarked on Theodore's 'eye for detail'.

"How do you do it, Theodore? I can give you any statue and you give me an exact duplicate. It's impossible to tell one from the other."

"I'm not a complicated man, Father. You give me something and I will imitate it pat down. I don't believe in adding things not already there. There was a reason why they weren't there in the first place and I'm not one to question that."

"Blind faith, Theo," Father Pinto replied. "Wish more people were like you. It would make my job easier." Then he added, "People say you are too rigid. I say you are a man of conviction. People don't have that today. They get sidetracked too easily." Father Pinto should know. Many a time he too lacked conviction and all the more admired Theodore's unflinching beliefs. At sermons, he regularly commented on Theodore being the epitome of a good Christian and cited his generosity in offering their church a six feet tall sculpture of the *Três Pessoas* free of charge.

It was while working on this cross that Theodore felt it was time to extend his large-heartedness to his family. He offered to build his only son, Dominic, a house in the family compound, near the jambolan tree.

Being a man to act upon his word, he rode his scooter past the local school and around the only oxymoron of the village, a triangular roundabout, as the locals called it, heading towards the panchayat to get that elusive No Objection Certificate.

"Mr Fernandes what brings you here? There is no gram sabha meeting today. Is it something to do with garbage, street lights, telephone lines?" asked the bewildered sarpanch Azgaonkar.

"No, nothing like that. This is personal."

"Personal?" hissed Azgaonkar.

"I'm thinking of building a small house for my son in my backyard. These are the plans and the papers. I would like to apply for an NOC, so work can begin. I've already got the architect's floor plans ... "

"You want an NOC?" Azgaonkar cut in eagerly.

"Mr Fernandes, see how many NOC applications are here on my desk. Everyone wants to build. Let me see your file and application. For you, I will do my best to give you an NOC sooner than later," he added with a smile.

As he flipped through the file, Azgaonkar recalled the many incidents when this man with the thin straight mouth had unrelentingly embarrassed him at gram sabha meetings. Now, it was going to be his turn.

Casually he looked up and remarked, "I hear you are building a large, special cross for the parish church, free of charge?"

"Yes. A small contribution to the community."

"I have an idea. You know from this year people cannot make plaster-of-Paris Ganeshas. It's a good thing to keep our wells, rivers and sea unpolluted. So I thought that our panchayat should have something special to set an example. You know we have paper Ganeshas in Goa. Very unique. And there's one village in Shiroda which has a wooden Ganesha. So I thought we should have a wooden Ganesha. It's different, no? Also, to show how eco-friendly we are, we can re-use old wood. What do you think?"

Without waiting for Theodore's answer, he continued, "There are many Hindu artisans who'll do it, but they don't have your eye for detail. I wanted to come to your house and ask you, but as if by destiny, you have come here. What do you think, Mr Fernandes? It will be a nice gesture of secularism, no? Moreover, we don't have to immerse it, so you don't have to worry about that. We will use it year after year ... all eco-friendly."

Theodore couldn't say anything. He'd heard one never gets an NOC without paying and he had come prepared to wait and fight the righteous battle. This demand however shifted the battle lines and left him no wriggle-space. If he refused, the people would call him anti-Hindu. If he did it, he would break his own vow to never carve idols. Hadn't he spent years fighting those images that beckoned to him from their wooden confines. Each time he'd waged battle against his desires, he had won. This time, too, it would be his victory.

Azgaonkar enjoyed watching Theodore's discomfort. 'Now where is all his conviction?' he thought. Like sandpaper, his words chaffed those carefully hewn beliefs that had directed Theodore's life. "It's only February, Mr Fernandes, there's time. Ganesha is a god who removes all obstacles. You should be honoured to carve his image."

Very slowly, so Theodore did not miss a thing, Azgaonkar closed the file and passed it to his assistant who with precision placed it at the bottom of the multi-coloured stack of files, so low that you could hear the metal clasps scratch the wooden desk.

The sarpanch looked past him and said, "Ah, Mrs Naik, your file is ready. Here it is." As the lady swished over to grab her coveted file, Alfred stood up and left.

As soon as Martha saw her husband walk in she knew something had changed. He walked with a perceptible stoop and instead of taking the side path around the house to his workshop, he went past her and into their bedroom. In their 34 years together Theodore never went into their bedroom except at night or when he was ill.

Martha thought he would snap out of it. While she constantly reprimanded him for his unyielding attitude, now she regretted the sudden change. He looked like a man defeated. As the coolness of February gave way to the heat of summer, the smell of ripening mangoes and fermenting cashews filled the somnolent afternoons. Meanwhile Martha filled with worry. Summer passed and the monsoon arrived and Theodore continued to spend hours under the jambolan tree recalling the swing he had made for Dominic. He remembered how on summer days they would spend hours collecting the dark purple fruit that splattered the ground. While he cut the fruit off the branches with a long stick topped with a sharp scythe, Dominic would run helter skelter collecting the fallen fruit. Many ended up in his belly. The rest Martha would give away to neighbours or make into a syrup which they drank through the summer days.

Then June arrived and it was San João. As usual, the village boys came around to plunge into their well. Dressed in short pants, vests and decked with kopells—wreaths of palm leaves and flowers worn on the head—they frolicked around the well waiting for Theodore to emerge and give them a bottle of feni. Martha kept glancing back at the shut door of the workshop as would the boys. Although they kept their smiles, they noticed that Theodore was nowhere in sight and soon started to grow a little apprehensive about that bottle of feni. Sensing the dampening mood, Martha quickly walked into the house and emerged with a bottle. The lingering youth thanked her, gulped down mouthfuls and carried on with their carousing.

Watching from his workshop, Theodore thought to himself, "Look at that, D'Souzas and Desais, dancing and dunking to celebrate a Christian saint. What a sight!" That night as Theodore closed the door to his workshop, it wasn't that familiar calm that met him on the other side. It was a furnace that burned within him. Over the past few days, he had fed it with the brittle brattle of years of dogma, guilt, anger, pain and now it raged.

Strangely the roiling made him feel alive. The memories and emotions he had stifled were now consuming him; and all the daily rituals which he fervently adhered to in the fear that if he didn't, he would lose control, were forgotten. He didn't go to church and he neglected the daily Angelus. He didn't bother about his weekly jaunts to the fish market, he skipped his cherished meals and most of all he stopped carving. He spent his hours imploding into the self stoked furnace, struggling with memories and fighting the pangs of guilt and remorse. Into this internal foundry, the image he had carved of himself was collapsing and he let himself fall into the empty space of nothingness.

Soon it was his granddaughter, little Esperanca's birthday. Father Pinto waddled to his seat and delicately draped his napkin over the bulge of his belly to prevent the sorpotel from staining his white robes. He noticed Theodore walk past carrying a plate stacked with food. Not wanting to interrupt his meal, Father Pinto stored the memory for a propitious moment.

The moment arrived. As his distended abdomen groaned under the duress of self indulgence, he requested Theodore to take him back to his quarters. Stepping out of the car, Father Pinto offered an embarrassed apology. "I overdid it today. I don't usually eat so much but your Martha is a great cook."

"I'm sure, Father. One of those days when you just have to let go."

"Yes, I guess so," said the weakly smiling priest, "For someone who doesn't let go, I couldn't help noticing your plate was also quite full."

"I was putting some food aside for our neighbours, the Sardessais. You know Margaret recently lost her husband, Raj. We'll go over later and give them the food. They were mourning and couldn't make it for the birthday."

"I heard about the accident. Very sad. You know what I always say? Everything happens for the best. When Margaret married into the Sardessai family she stopped coming to church. May be now in her pain she will think of returning to Christ. Anyway, thank you Theodore. God bless."

Theodore was taken aback by Father Pinto's comment. As he watched him, he wished he had a pin. That would be a funny sight, to see the padre uncontrollably squiggle across the church yard like a punctured balloon.

Theodore smiled to himself and felt a weight lift off. In the widening space he recalled growing up with his neighbour and best friend, Raj. He remembered how they celebrated festivals together, how they ate at each others house. "When Our Lady came to our house they all came and prayed with us," Theodore recalled. "And when Ganesha was brought to their house, we visited and ate with them, lit crackers and had so much fun. We never thought twice about who was Hindu or Catholic. Then I changed. I lost my childhood too early. I had to work to support my mother and five kids. I became so much like my father—rigid and strict. I thought it was the way to be. Raj always asked me— What's wrong with you? You've changed so much."

"He was my best friend but he no longer seemed to fit into my world and like everything that didn't fit in, I ignored him. Ignored people, things, emotions, my own thoughts, thinking that if I didn't pay them attention, they would go away. They didn't. They kept gazing at me from the grains and textures of the wood I held in my hands. They were the ghosts of myself I was denying. 'Carve me,' they said. I failed my purpose. If I had carved them I would have released them and consequently myself."

Theodore rushed home and looked through his pieces of wood. That's when he saw it, the features of an elephant with four arms swirling in the tight knots and contours of the block of rosewood. He plunged into work, not as a sculptor but as a facilitator enabling the elephant god to emerge from this hardwood prison, to smile and dance.

He hammered, chiselled and shaped wood into a 3-feet tall standing Ganesha.

There was no poignancy of feature, or fall of garment too difficult to carve. His hands and tools flowed like molten liquid etching rich robes and intricate florals. The trunk of Ganesha was delicately curved and as if poised in the stance of a dancer, Ganesha's pot-bellied body emerged to display an easy, graceful double-bend dvibhanga pose.

That very evening Theodore wrapped the statue in a cloth and drove to Azgaonkar's house. He placed it on the dining table and like a magician swished off the veil. The final sculpture was indeed a beauty, brimming with intensity. Ganesha stood there in splendour as the god of abundance that he was. His eyes glowed, his smile welcomed and each of his four arms endowed the gifts of protection, fearlessness, abundance and blessings for new beginnings. As Ganesh Chaturthi approached, Theodore found himself visiting the pandal everyday. His work was displayed on an elaborate stage surrounded by sparkling lights and bhajans blared from multi-storied speakers.

Azgaonkar licked his wounded pride as he signed Theodore's NOC. The sculptor meanwhile sat in quiet contentment, gazing out of the window, watching the streaming lines of people bow before their beloved god and he felt that familiar calm settle on him. This time it felt natural, soft and ethereal and slowly filled all of him. A gentle curve of a smile lit up his face for he could see images of life everywhere and he thought to himself, "Now, how am I going to keep all this abundance simple?"

'The Homecoming' won the first prize at the Fundação Oriente Short Story Competition 2011.

Not So Feeble
Bevinda Collaço

I can see myself in her eyes. That is why I hate sponge baths. I see that pleat of distaste between her nostril and lip. Through that pleat I can get inside her Nurse head. I can see what she is seeing. Loose crêpey skin drooping dismally from bones, like a balloon that has lost its air, sagging against the pillows and water mattress.

I have grown used to the water bed. Used to feel sea-sick on it initially; now, with the marvellous adaptability of all living things, even at ninety-one, I have adapted. It prevents bed sores they said and bed sores are a bad thing. The sponge is held against my back and she rubs me down like she's rubbing a horse. Brittle bones, cadela! Brittle bones, bitch! I'm snarling at her in my head.

What she ignores are dull eyes barely blinking and a slack mouth with a little drool down the corners. She scrubs my front and the water goes all over the place. Not a good feeling. Push, pull, turn, yank, rub. In five minutes she's done. Dried, powdered, dressed, rolled to the left while she makes one half of the bed, rolled to the right while she makes the other half. Brings me some pap she calls breakfast and I can feel the hard cold spoon against my gums as she forces the crap in. I swallow. I have to. There's nothing else to do. She's shoving the next spoonful in. She feeds me tea in a spoon then scrubs my mouth dry. Dab, cadela, dab, at ninety-one the skin hurts.

I want to scream at her and kick her out on her fat butt, but no. The worst humiliation is yet to come. She rolls my gown up and slides the bed pan under me, covering the whole tableau with a sheet. She opens the door to take the breakfast things down. Ah, divine respite. I can get on with my favourite past time. Listen to the sounds of the house and figure out what's going on where, and shitting, of course. If I don't she'll just leave the frigging bedpan there until I do.

The house is stirring. My younger daughter Marguerida is a grandmother at sixty. She enjoys her children and her grandchildren. Her daughter is twenty-seven. And her daughter's children are three and one. Four generations in one house. Ah, but it's a big house in a still green corner of Goa, originally a farmhouse in forty acres of flat land, a river and a hill. The town has crept all around us but we keep them at bay with our plantations of cashew and that beautiful betel nut. I can see banana trees, some drumstick trees, jackfruit trees, and know every one of the papaya trees and vegetable patches. There's pepper growing around the betel nut trees and lots of pineapples. There's this monkey that sits on the chickoo tree holding her baby. She comes to visit me, I think, as she stares at me while solemnly grooming her baby.

She reminds me of Mallika. There's no real resemblance really, because Mallika looked like an ebony queen and this monkey does not. Even at eighty-two Mallika carries herself like a queen, slim, tall, now white-haired. She worked as my housemaid for many years before moving to Canacona to marry a good-for-nothing farmer. He died. Apparently he smoked in bed and one afternoon after drinking heavily his bed caught fire and he burnt to death. Mallika was working in the fields. Even though he used to beat her, she was inconsolable. I went there and brought her back with me. Since then she's been a member of my household and now lives as an honoured guest.

Not So Feeble

I know she has something to tell me, but we never get any time alone. Too many visitors, too many people wanting to confess their past and present indiscretions. What is it about a bedridden comatose vegetable that makes them want to vomit all that is dark and dirty? Is it because they think I will carry their secrets to my grave? That I cannot hear them? Actually I can hear every word spoken, sometimes even those that are not spoken.

I wonder what Mallika wants to unburden.

There are kokam trees with the large red sweet and sour fruits that make curries so heavenly. I sometimes smell that mouthwatering curry but all I can do is drool. The nurse in consultation with the bedpan decides what I can and cannot eat. There were many, many years when I could eat anything. Correction. I could never bring myself to eat frog legs. Only here in Goa they call it 'Jumping Chicken'. Not because I love frogs. I think they are repulsive creatures, which is why the thought of eating any part of them gives me the creeps. Funny how memories become so clear at ninety-one. I rather like it. There's a whole arena of activity behind these vacant eyes and slack mouth. I can move in that space, taking giant leaps through time. I take a giant leap now.

I feel a coiled stillness, like a steel spring held tight, very tight. A skinny brown hand holds a fat round kokam fruit. We called it 'binda'. It's not the deep burgundy colour that is plucked and used to make a juice concentrate, or seasoning for curries, or fertiliser, but the bright red that still needs to ripen. I know that it will be too sour, but my hand brings the berry close to my lips.

I am in my own skin eighty years ago in my grandfather's fields, waiting for my cousin Fernando to come looking for me. I bite into the taut skin and God in Heaven it's so sour I can feel my eyebrows trying to crawl inside my mouth. My eleven-year-old face is wrinkled horribly as the sour flesh and juice explodes. I shudder in delight and take another bite. A twig cracks and I'm off. Like a bullet from a gun.

There was a certain purity to running in the fields in our village. Each desperate lungful of fresh sparkling air, a thin urgent body leaning into the wind and thin strong brown limbs thrusting hard against the flimsy barrier of a faded cotton dress, arms pumping wildly, running, running, running. Flying down the terraced brown paddy fields; feet barely touching the sharp stubble of the harvested crop. Hard on her heels flew her cousin Fernando and behind him some more of the clan. Why did they run so much when they were children? No one was chasing them. They ran because they could. There was no other reason.

She skidded to a halt under a spreading mango tree and flung herself down biting into the sour sweet explosion of the red binda. Face twisted in horrible ecstasy, Frieda looked into the distance as cousin Fernando slammed down in the cool earth next to her. She handed him a red binda from her pocket.

"This is a sour one," he observed, panting.

"They're the best," she said. "The dark ones are for old women." He bit into the binda. As the sour juice squirted in his mouth he flung himself back on the ground and kicked his legs in the air.

"It tho thar!" he screamed, laughing and gagging. She smiled absently. The rest of the cousins trotted up and sat solemnly around them.

"Why're you sitting here?" demanded eight-year-old Tiny Tony. "Come down to the river, we'll catch some fish for the nuns."

They raced down the narrow mud road which wound its way to the river between low red laterite stone walls. Laterite bricks look soft with all those spongy holes in them, but they are as hard as the iron that is found in them. They even hide all sorts of insects, even scorpions, ready to attack the unwary bottom that rests on the wall. But Frieda and her cousins were not afraid of scorpions or any creepy crawlies.

No, they were not afraid of most things but they were all afraid of The Tree. No running this time. Each tried to walk slower than the other when the giant tree with red flags all over it appeared around the bend. There were joss sticks at the base of the tree, small idols and vermillion and yellow powder.

They took this all in through the corners of their eyes as they walked stiff-legged towards the tree. The air was strangely silent, as if all Nature was holding its breath. Like them. They walked on making as little sound as possible, mouths dry, eyes unblinking. They reached the tree and shivered in the distinct coolness under its huge canopy.

Suddenly a gust of wind soughed through the leaves and a bird twittered. As one unit, the children flew forward, gasping for breath, running as if ten devils were after them. They ran without stopping until they reached the sluice gates. Frieda and Fernando did not say a word to each other. They waded into the clear water of the river, grabbing a broken basket from the river bank and—the Tree forgotten—set about the serious business of catching fish.

You could catch fish with a bamboo stick, a length of twine and a tiny barbed hook bought at the village *posro*, which was baited with a piece of prawn. Prawn made excellent bait, especially for catfish. But it was risky using a fishing rod to catch catfish, especially when you had to take it off the hook. All catfish have a defense mechanism of spines that lock into place so that they stick outwards. This can inflict severe wounds on the unwary. Like Porquito. He was a local boy who was loved by all these cousins on holiday in the village. He was always laughing, ready for adventure and a practical joker. He was also very brave.

Porquito's real name was Pedro Vicente Sebastian Theodore Britto de Braganza. He had caught a large catfish, all of ten inches long. He held the wriggling fish triumphantly and grasped it firmly to take it off the hook. But the fish had other ideas and sank its bony spine into the fleshy part of Porquito's palm. Of course the cousins sprang to help and tried pulling out the fish, but it only thrust deeper and Porquito was in agony because a catfish also has venom.

A fisherman walking past had looked enquiringly at the huddle of children. He disappeared into a small boat house and returned unhurriedly with a bottle of feni, Goa's fiery liquor which is used for everything, from medicine and seasoning to entertainment and ritual. He spread open Porquito's hand on the ground with the fish still sitting smugly in it. Placing his calloused foot on Porquito's fingers, he grasped the fish firmly and yanked it out with a sickening *chirrrik*. Porquito's scream sent the birds flying out of the trees. The fisherman then uncorked the bottle of feni and poured a liberal amount into the jagged wound left by the fish spine. Porquito whimpered. The fisherman placed his hand on Porquito's head and patted him lightly, calling him a brave boy. He corked his bottle, turned around and walked back to the boat shed to stash his magic potion.

After that there was a special bond between Porquito, the cousins and the fisherman, whose name was Mogu. He was tall and spare, with a dark brown hairless velvet body covered only with a loincloth called a *kashtti*. He lived in a tiny shack with his tiny daughter Mallika. They called him Mogubab out of deep respect and he taught them about the river, the mangroves, the fish, how to leave the fat females alone because they had eggs and needed to spawn.

He taught Frieda and her cousins where they could wade safely and where the river was deep. He taught them how to fish with a rod, with a net and with a basket. They absorbed every word in rapt attention. Above all, he taught them how to sail a canoe and allowed them to borrow his whenever they wished, on condition that they did not go further than the bend in the river.

Mallika, not yet two at that time, was fascinated by Frieda. She would sit quietly, gravely studying her every move.

Fernando and Tiny Tony waded in the river, sending the fish towards Frieda sitting motionless in the water with her basket. Exactly three fish swam into the basket and she sprang up with them leaping in the afternoon sunlight. She caught two more, then another one.

The Sisters of Charity were loved by one and all in the village. They were different from the stiff and starched nuns at Frieda's convent school in Bombay. These wore blue bordered saris for one thing and moved briskly up and down the village, giving people medicines, treating wounds, and sometimes just visiting those living alone to share some cheery news or help out with the household chores. Frieda and her cousins had reason to visit the convent often to get bites, cuts and scratches tended to.

Their relationship with the nuns began with Fernando's Cycle Incident. One morning Fernando decided to ride a bicycle with no brakes down a slope. He ended up with the cycle in a gutter and with a couple of deep gashes on his arm and leg. The nuns gave him a tetanus shot, carefully stitched him up and said they'd check the wound after two days. The cousins had decided to do a spot of fishing first to feed their meagre catch to their grandfather's scrawny cat Bartholomiaow. One nun said hesitantly, "If you don't mind very much, could you give us the fish? We don't have any in the House and it would be nice ..."

And just like that, the Convent became a regular stop after every fishing expedition ... Frieda looked dreamily into the distance, someone was stroking her hand. It was Mallika, the fisherman's little daughter.

It was Mallika. *Beautiful, ebony-skinned silver-haired right-hand of mine who worked so hard despite orders to stop and could laugh like a child. She was speaking softly and insistently,* "Frieda bai, I know you can hear me and I know you can see me, I have to tell you my story and you tell me what to do. I will ask you a question; you press my hand once if your answer is 'yes'. If your answer is 'no', do nothing. Can you do that?"

Trust Mallika to give me a brain teaser on my death bed and push me to do stupid things. Something was eating at her. I pressed her hand. She chuckled softly, "You lie there like you're dead and they all think you cannot see or hear, that is why they all confess their sins to you. You know everything, don't you?" *I pressed once.*

"Does Marguerida know?" *Why should I tell her everything? My daughter also knew I could see and hear and it tickled her hugely, but it amused me to let Mallika think only she knew this delightful secret. My fingers stayed limply in her hand.*

"Good," she said, "I'll tell you my story. I told you my husband used to beat me, but carefully never on my hands or face, so that no one could see the bruises?" *Pressed once.*

"Well he began taking me out of the house up into the orchard and there he would beat me, so no one would hear." *I pressed her hand in shock.*

She continued, stroking my hand and in a dreamy voice continued, "It became more and more difficult for me to do any house work or field work. He even broke two ribs and one day he gathered a leaf full of red ants and thrust it down my blouse. He laughed so much. That was when I decided I had to kill him before he killed me. Are you shocked?" *My hand lay limply in hers.*

"He used to make me pour his drinks for him, so I poured him stiffer drinks than usual, that afternoon. I also dropped two sleeping tablets in. He lit a cigarette to smoke it but fell asleep and it fell to the floor.

"I stubbed it out and waited for ten minutes. When he was in a heavy deep sleep, I lit the cigarette, inhaled once, then twice. His arm was on the pillow near his face. I placed the lit cigarette on the pillow. I sat on a chair and watched him burn. I wanted him to open his eyes and see that I had done this, but he did not wake up. When the flames spread all over the bed, I slipped out of the back door and went to work in our fields.

"The neighbours saw the smoke coming out of our house. Some tried to put the fire out; others came to bring me news of the fire. I flew to the house, screaming that my husband was sleeping inside; it was blazing by now. My neighbours restrained me, but I needed to go and see for myself that that devchar was really burnt to death. They would not let me go in even though I kicked and screamed and wept and tore my hair.

"The police came in later, with the fire engine. They were shocked. He was completely burnt they said and yes, dead. Was he smoking a cigarette when he went to sleep, they asked me. The relief was so great; I crumpled to the ground unconscious. It has been eating at me all these years. Did I do the right thing, bai? Tell me! Did I do the right thing?"

She had kept that secret for more than thirty years. She sighed a long sigh and wept softly, her tears bathing my hand clasping hers. Tightly.

The Vessel

Sharon Soares

As I closed the twelfth page of the newspaper and turned to keep it aside, my eyes welled up. My tears spilled over and fell on the newspaper ... wetting the photograph on the obituary.

Everyone has to go some day, but when someone familiar is gone, those close to the departed are shaken up. I brushed my tears away and gripped my half empty mug of coffee with both hands.

DEATH ... Jesoin D ... expired peacefully ... funeral cortege will leave this evening ...

I better call home and inform them, I thought. As I reached the phone, it rang.

"Hello mama! I was about to call you up. I'm okay. Yes, Terence is at work. I was having breakfast when I read of Jesoin. Will you be going for the funeral?"

"I wanted to go, but I have a hair cutting appointment today, I can't miss that. I may go some other day to offer condolences. Don't worry if you can't make it either. Anyway, other than her son, who else knows us?"

The Vessel

So many years had passed since that incident, but it wasn't easy to change Mother's mind. I did not say anything.

"I want to go for her funeral. This is the final farewell. I have to go. Alright then ... Tell Daddy I asked about him."

It's been nearly a year since Daddy has been bedridden. Otherwise he would have come along with me. He would surely not have missed Jesoin's funeral.

It is very quiet at my house. I like it that way. As I rocked in my armchair, thoughts of Jesoin beckoned me, like the rabbit in *Alice in Wonderland*. When I was a child she would clasp me in her arms and rock me to sleep.

She truly had magic in her hands. She could outdo any of the best chefs with her cooking. Whenever I attended any event, as I tasted the food I would always think of her. Daddy would say, "We have never tasted sorpotel to match Jesoin's, and to accompany that, her succulent sannas ... I just can't stop eating them."

Daddy and I would always praise her cooking. She would be delighted. Her husband was a drunkard, her son was still young, and there was no one to say a kind word to her. I would mischievously say, "Look, the praise has swelled you up like a pappad." She would blush even more.

She would work very diligently and earnestly on every chore. Ever since I was born, she would come daily to our house to work.

Mother would sometimes taunt us, "Yes, you only want her food. If one uses good oil and tasty masalas why won't the food taste delicious?"

It is rightly said, you must not praise a woman too much in front of another woman. According to Mother, her food was so-so and there was nothing special about it. It was okay just to fill the belly. If there was any party or occasion or feast at home, Mother would take charge of the kitchen.

Jesoin would quietly follow all her instructions. She had to chop and cook as per Mother's orders. She had to chop carrot and potato 'cubes' in the same way for stew, and she had to slice onion and potato finely for pulao. But even then, Mother would drop into the kitchen and scold her without any reason. Jesoin's voice would rarely be heard.

"Mama, let Jesoin cook cafreal for the party."

"Why? Don't I know how to cook cafreal? I have prepared the masala for it. Let her cook some other time." But I knew that Mother would never let Jesoin cook for a party.

Daddy would say, "Jesoin is an asset for us, she has the all best qualities of a cook. May she always serve us like this, may God bless her."

"Where else will she go, Daddy? She has taken care of me since birth. This is her life. From morning to evening she works here and then goes to her home, to serve them."

She was always smiling. She was well built and would always dress neatly. She owned only a few dresses but they were in good taste—simple pleated cotton dresses that suited her well. She wore a fine necklace with a 'J' locket pendant that had a scapular devoutly entwined around it.

She would walk with great strides. When she picked me up from school, I would have to trot briskly alongside her as she walked carrying my school bag and water bottle.

One day I picked up some other classmate's stickers and put them in my bag. On the way home I told Jesoin. She told me gently, "Ina bai, you have not done the right thing. God has given you everything—a good father and mother, a lovely house and lots of toys. Then why did you take that child's things without telling her? Jesus will feel very sad because of this. What will you do now?"

"I ... okay ... I will return the stickers tomorrow."

The Vessel

The next evening, I found the same kind of stickers on my table. Jesoin had bought them with her own money. This was my Jesoin!

That year, I remember Jesoin's birthday—that fateful day. She had lovingly brought us food cooked from her home.

"Baba, today is my birthday. I have brought you beef assad cooked on a wood fire. And a small bebinca, baked on coals."

"Really? It's been ages since I ate food cooked on a wood fire. This is all very tasty. Your ingredients are perfect. The bebinca melts in my mouth. And it looks so good, one layer over the other. Well done!" Daddy was delighted.

"You have served us a feast on your birthday, Jesoin!" I exclaimed. She had neatly laid out the assad and bebinca on the table.

Mother returned early from work that day.

"Why is the food served on the table today?" she asked. We would normally serve ourselves in the kitchen on weekdays.

"Celi, today is Jesoin's birthday. Did you forget? She has brought us food cooked from home."

"And this casserole?" Mother was staring at the vessel containing the beef dish.

"She brought it from her home," Daddy replied.

"From home? I have been searching like mad for this vessel. Susan had gifted us this vessel for our wedding, don't you remember?"

"No ..."

"She must have taken it home. Or did she steal it? I will ask her right now. Jesoin, what did you take this home for? And you bring it back after so long?"

"Bai, what are you saying?"

"Yes, this house is in your hands, isn't it? You do as you wish here."

Daddy and I were shocked. Jesoin's face wilted like a faded rose.

"Celi, what is the matter? Let it be now. Let us eat," said my father.

"I don't want to eat. Tell me, Jesoin, when did you take this vessel?"

"Bai, this vessel is mine."

"What? Would you have this kind of a vessel? Since when did you start buying Cook and Serve vessels? You stole it!"

"Bai ..."

Mother did not allow her to say another word. She stormed off in a rage.

"Jesoin, don't be upset with Celi's words. She has come home tired from work. Something must have happened there and she has taken it out on you."

"Baba, I am not a thief ..."

She left that day and never returned. Today, after all those years, I would see her again—in a coffin.

I had tried to convince Mother, to defend Jesoin. How could a woman who taught me good morals, not to steal, actually do something like this herself?

But Mother never forgave her. She would only get angrier. And Jesoin never came back.

Only a letter came from her some days later:

"Dear Celia bai, Eusebio bab and my beloved Ina bai,

I worked at your house for many years. I never asked for a raise. Bab Eusebio never gave me cause to do so, he

The Vessel

always paid me well. Many people tempted me to work for more money elsewhere, but I stayed loyal to you.

It was my job to fill the plates of this house, and by those same plates I have earned my living. Then how could I ever betray you? That too for a cooking vessel? Never!

God has destined my hands for a special cause—to cook good food, not to steal. I fill vessels with my food, so that they may be eaten from and wiped clean, not to hoard them in my possession. Celia bai, please keep that vessel. If you still feel that I have stolen it from your kitchen, I cannot prove my innocence any further.

What is a vessel? If you go to the market, so many different kinds of vessels are available there. If you have money, you can buy any vessel, but a person's self respect is not for sale. I will always love all of you, but I cannot work for you anymore. The accusation of theft is a heavy one. If anything happens in the future, you will always suspect me. So of my own wish, and for my own self respect, I am leaving this job.

Celia bai, I had bought that vessel with my own money, after collecting the tips that Eusebio bab gave me. I had gone to Bombay just once, when His Holiness the Pope had come, in 1986. I have no proof of this. You may well say that seeing you going to Bombay for shopping, that I have made up this lie. God knows my heart and mind. Jesus is in half of my name, then why would I break the Fifth Commandment? Someday you will know the truth. I hope you realise this when I am alive.

I will find it hard to meet you in person. My heart will become heavy, my knees will tremble and my eyes will fill with tears. In such a state I will not be able to speak. That is why I have written this letter.

Yours, Jesoin."

On reading the letter, Mother's suspicions only grew stronger. What could Daddy and I do?

After a few days, a new maid from Karnataka came to work. Mother showed her around the kitchen and taught her how to cook Goan food, but there was something missing in the food. Jesoin's love? Or the true Goan flavour?

The maid left in two years and another replaced her. But there was no one like Jesoin.

The phone rang, shaking me from my thoughts of Jesoin.

"Mother, what is the matter? Why are you crying? Is Daddy okay?"

"Ina, I have been mistaken. May God forgive me ... May Jesoin forgive me ..."

"What has happened? Mama?"

"Ina, do you remember that vessel ... Jesoin ... the theft ... that vessel has been at Susan's place all these years."

"What!"

"I myself had sent a dish in that vessel to Susan. In their haste when leaving for Canada, she forgot about returning it. I too forgot. She came to Goa last week. She visited our home today after many years. I was shocked to see the vessel. Poor Jesoin is gone ... Bai, please would you please take me with you for her funeral?"

Originally written in Konkani as 'Aidonn'. Translated by José Lourenço.

Symbiosis
Sheela Jaywant

A board near The International Centre at Dona Paula points to 'Machado's Cove'. Narrow lanes crookedly find their way to the banks of the river Zuari below. The area resembles any residential colony in the newer localities of growing Indian towns like Ghaziabad near Delhi, or Nashik in neighbouring Maharashtra or even the outskirts of Guwahati in the Far East. Oversized, ostentatious bungalows ('villa' is the new word for bungalow these days) squeeze out every permitted square foot to build upon. Some have two floors, some three. Most have sloping roofs to deal with the heavy rains here. Their ornate gates are unexceptional. Garishly painted walls chew up the edges of the grit-surfaced, badly scarred roads. Adolescent trees, standing awkwardly at irregular intervals, strive to stretch their sickly, lanky limbs towards the azure sky. Come monsoons, they get covered in baby leaves. Post October, they are stark again.

The difference between the architectural mongrels in other States and Goa is that these are the 'second' or holiday homes of the rich from cities like Delhi, Ahmedabad or

Mumbai. Their owners, the 'landlords', seldom live in them, though their relatives and friends occasionally come to stay during the holiday season or over weekends. A few villas are tenanted by people who have jobs in nearby Panaji. The majority are generally kept locked, unless briefly rented out, and looked after by 'caretakers' (no one uses the word servant any longer) like Bhadoor and his family, who live on the premises in tiny, independent sheds called 'quarters'. Plots without caretakers can be identified by the piles of unattended garbage dumped in them. 'Bhadoor' is a colloquial corruption of the name Bahadur; every watchman or servant is Bhadoor, irrespective of his real name.

In bygone years, one tracked an address by mentioning the name of a house-owner; for example: "... take a left at Babu Naik's house ..." Later, numbered plots in sectored blocks made it easier to give directions. But even now many people give directions using landmarks instead of numbers: "... take a left at the pink villa after the pharmacy next to the chapel."

Rarely does anyone get lost though, thanks to the mobile phone. Everyone has one, even a servant (sorry, caretaker) like Bhadoor, who cleans and maintains four villas and their gardens. Every other month he gets a call from one or other of the landlords, checking on payments of bills, or telling him to be hospitable to some friends who would be holidaying there during so and so days. He gets his salaries on time, a couple of thousands per kothi (that's 'villa' in servant-lingo) per month. He doesn't need to moonlight any longer.

Back in the 'eighties, when most of the kothis hadn't been built and he didn't have an election card, Bhadoor used to earn some extra bucks cutting onions at the choris-pao, sausage-and-bread stall. Today this snack, like the beef cutlet, is obsolete: most of the owners and visitors are non-beef-pork-eating. Even the mention of such meats is blasphemy. What flourishes is bhel, the Mumbai version of Delhi's savoury roadside snack, chaat. To eat xit-kodi, the Goan staple meal of curry and rice, one has to go to Panaji.

One solitary stall tucked in the centre of the colony does good business selling rajma-chawal—red kidney-beans and rice—a cheap, filling and nutritious meal. The stall is actually a caretaker's quarters being misused. The owner of that property hasn't been here in years and, unchallenged, that caretaker, now considered an established entrepreneur rather than a trespasser, has taken possession of a chunk of the plot and employed migrant lads to do 'home-delivery'. His fare is as popular with workers as it is with 'guests'—the visitors who come on holidays.

The arrival of a 'guest' is preceded by a flurry of activity in and around a kothi. Caretaker-belongings lying around in the kitchen, veranda or bathroom are removed. Bhadoor is very particular that no signs of his children's clothes, shaving-samaan or trinkets are visible anywhere. Then, windows are opened, the garden is weeded, furniture dusted, the fridge stocked with drinking water, the linen aired. 'The Visit' seldom lasts for more than four days. Longer visits are welcomed because they mean a higher tip at departure.

This latest SMS has upset Bhadoor's family. He reads it out yet again to his wife, Sundari. His daughter, Resham, echoes the words to her brothers, Rajoo and Guddoo, who snatch the phone from him to read the message for themselves.

In the thirty years that Bhadoor has lived in these 'quarters', the owners have made rare but meticulous forays to check on their property. In the other three villas where Bhadoor works, the quarters are used as store-rooms and kept locked. (Rumours abound, not without reason, that unoccupied 'open' quarters attract pimps and rogues).

"Malik-malkin are going to stay here for the pooraay mahino? For a whole month? Chaay. Bad news."

"Could be zyaada. Maybe longer. It seems malik has retired and malkin wants to stay hinga. She loves the baareesh." Malik means lord or boss. His wife is thus malkin.

"Why? Isn't there paoos in the rest of the muluk? Doesn't it rain in the rest of the country? In Delhi? What will happen to us? Where are we going to sukhao the kapdey, dry the clothes?"

"Drying clothes is the least of our problems. Mummy, Guddoo and the four of us will have to sleep in one kholi. In a single room, think of that. Aadat choot gayee; we aren't used to it any longer."

The servants (sorry, caretakers) in and around Dona Paula speak an indigenous mix of many tongues: Hindi, Marathi, English, Nepali, Kannada and Konkani. The vocabulary is restricted and at first it sounds familiar but incomprehensible; one gets used to the accent and words within a day. It's a dialect that has evolved and is used right down through Nagalim till Taleigao's Sao Paulo market and beyond till St Cruz. Catch a bus from the Ferry to the University and you'll hear all versions of it: some sprinkled with Rajasthani, some with Malayalam. For two generations of bhailley, 'outsiders' who have settled here, the quarrel over standardization of the Konkani script and status is irrelevant. They have borrowed words and incorporated them into their own mother-tongues. The migrant labourers' interdependency for survival has blended several languages. Each gardener, small-stall-owner, sweeper and coolie has added something to this fusion. Sharing of resources—plumbing and carpentry tools, water, rents—has led to a shared lexicon. Abuses lead to quarrels, or vice-versa, as do the use of toilets and stolen job opportunities. The nameless language that has been distilled from those experiences, effective and accepted by locals, politicians, businessmen and labourers alike, is the one that Bhadoor's children speak.

"Hari is coming baygeen. Maybe phalya-para. He'll be here in a dees or two, for his naukri. He's got a job offer, and we said he could stay hinga, here with us, remember?" Hari is a village-mate from far off Bihar.

Bhadoor's house has been (still is) the platform from which many young men like Hari have sought their fortune. In the last twenty-seven years, as many lads have brought their brides, found themselves in quarters like Bhadoor's and settled here to raise their families. In time, their children will follow Bhadoor's children's example and bring roshani, glory, to them. They will cook and procreate in a single-room shed, but will make use of the vacant verandas of the villa to sleep through velvet summer afternoons and tropical nights abuzz with the malaria-macchars. They will get used to running water and 'flushes' in toilets. They will dream, aspire, succeed.

Bhadoor barks: "No one can stay with us whilst the malik-malkin are here. We'll make some other arrangements for Hari. I'll ask Jabbar if his kholi is free. I could pay him some money. Hari can repay me later. Now ... Sundari, get the place clean by today. None of our things, ek bhi cheez nahin, should be seen here. Samajhi na? Am I clear?"

Sundari whimpers and slinks away, duster and broom in hand. But Rajoo, the eldest, is quivering to snap. Where will he park his bhel-puri cart? He's invested in it with the money he's saved from his job as a scuba-diving helper at a five-star resort.

"Take it to someone else's compound for a couple of days," Bhadoor tells him. "Be discreet."

Rajoo curses audibly under his breath.

Bhadoor sternly reminds him: "This isn't our ghar. It's the malik's home. If someone tattles to him that we're parking your cart here, we could get thrown out."

Rajoo-Guddoo-Resham consider the villa their home. They have played and slept in the rooms on the ground floor— perhaps with caution, yet without qualms.

Guddoo, who sells zips to tailors and purse-makers, reasons: " ... Rajoo, when the malik or malkin are here, I have to find a place for my things, too."

"I hate staying in quarters."

Resham pipes in: "It's free, no rent, remember?"

The pragmatic Resham is a self-trained beautician. She goes to her clients' homes to cut hair, apply henna, wax limbs, massage feet ... charging much less than her competitors. She has picked up a smattering of English from her foreign customers, and learnt to be hygienic and meticulous. Like her bhais, her elder brothers, she is ambitious and wishes to have her own shop. Unlike them, she is not rough. Silently, tidily, she places in a plastic bucket, hairdriers, brushes of various shapes and bristles, long-handled combs, clips, small towels, an array of bottles and jars, spatulas, and other paraphernalia. This corner of the kitchen of the villa is hers. When visitors come a-holidaying she moves her things back into the quarters.

Bhadoor allows her to keep the chavi, the key to the backdoor of the kothi which leads into the kitchen. He trusts her. She won't misuse anything. She sometimes drinks cold water from the fridge, but that, most people agree, is allowed. Resham secretly gives the key to her brothers if they want to use the bathroom for a hot shower or a fancy shave, maybe once or twice a week.

The siblings don't dare use the bedrooms or the cupboards like some of the other caretakers' children. Bhadoor would thrash them to bits if they did.

Today, Resham refuses to give Guddoo the key. "Not when malik is expected. Ask Bapuji," she says.

Sundari, still whining and grumbling, is half-heartedly sweeping the drive and portico.

Until malik and malkin return to Delhi, Bhadoor will have to make arrangements for his sons and Resham. Surreptitiously, of course; if they get caught staying in another villa's quarters without the knowledge of that landlord, there could be a police case. His livelihood depends on trust and his reputation on word of mouth.

He overhears snippets of conversation and discovers that his family has not been obeying him as they should.

Sundari: "The gas cylinder is almost empty. Hurry up, book one. And go and buy some kerosene and collect some wood. We have to start the choola for ourselves. Hai Ram, I've got a headache ." So, Sundari has used the gas, then, sometimes.

Resham: "Shouldn't we clean the house first? They'll be here in two days. We can't leave any nishaani, any signs of us, right?"

An agitated Bhadoor wonders, which nishaanis? Where? Why? How?

As if in answer, he hears her say: "We haven't used their things, we haven't slept on their beds. Our mattresses and chattaees we can roll up and carry back to the quarters."

He sighs, relieved. Then wonders again, were the A.C. or fans ever used? The electricity bill would give them away.

Rajoo: "The bathroom on the ground floor has my bottle of perfumed hair-oil on the sill."

Guddoo: "I hope you didn't touch anything else ... malik notices the levels of the shampoo and after-shave and ...

everything, everything."

Rajoo: "You mean the daroo? Haven't even smelled the whiskey."

Resham: "The fridge has to be cleaned. Go buy the eggs, butter, milk, tea, sugar. I'll check the bathrooms, windows, washing-machine. Go."

Bhadoor is afraid. If his family has used what belongs to the kothi, if they get thrown out ... the monsoons are unforgiving to the unsheltered ... besides, there's no going back to his village in far-off Bihar. His children have no memories of it. His own are diluted and remote.

Once, about five years ago, malik discovered that they had been using the 'landline'. The bill had the numbers on it. They got away with one big tantrum, several nagging reminders of the incident, plus a deduction from their salary.

After that, they have been careful. Or so Bhadoor has believed until now.

Contrary to the meaning of his name, the Brave One, Bhadoor today, unusually, is afraid to know the truth. Keep quiet, and the troubles will go away.

Routinely, for a small commission, a taxi-driver friend is informed to pick up guests from Vasco or Karmali and then show them the sights, take them shopping and dining through the duration of their stay. Bhadoor and his wife keep the guests comfortable whist the trio, Rajoo-Guddoo-Resham stay away.

Can't question the children now, Bhadoor figures. They're grown up. He hopes his family will be responsible enough to not sully his name.

The day malik-malkin arrive, the trio is nowhere to be seen.

Later, Guddoo phones Bhadoor: "We have rented a hut on the slope." On the other side of the Bambolim plateau, where the road sharply skids down to the Taleigaon fields, there are big buildings with hundreds of apartments.

"We'll manage the rent," Guddoo assures him, "We have our jobs. Also, Rajoo and I can wash cars. Resham can get more clients here." Bhadoor is relieved, and proud of his offspring.

The crowded hutment skirting the road is encircled by smelly slush, unlike the cleaner surroundings of the colony. Still, it's a place where there's no bhook-bali, where a person can earn his bread.

For the entire month Bhadoor-Sundari slog. They clean the water-tanks, execute a new layout for the garden, and shop, chop, sweep and mop till their sinews ache. The blank hours are spent in the kitchen, standing or squatting, waiting, waiting, waiting to be called ... to make tea or search for some long-forgotten curio or 'hurry-up and start cooking' for yet another noisy, drunken dinner with faces both new and familiar.

Two days before his departure, the malik hands over a sheaf of papers to Bhadoor.

"Xerox copies," he says. "I've sold this place. Someone will come to collect these."

"A new malik? Bhadoor asks, trembling, hesitant: "What about us? Where will we go? What will we do? The monsoons ... this place, this shed behind the kothi is the only home we've known."

"How can I say? The new owner will decide. He may want someone else. You're old, Bhadoor, you should retire. You've been loyal and good to me. Here, take this." He gives him enough cash to tide him over six months.

Sundari weeps silently when he tells her what has happened. They are just a twenty minute walk away from the children, but they prefer to use the phone to give them the news. Resham gets emotional, but the boys say: "You always said it isn't our home, Bapuji. We can all stay in this hut here. We'll manage."

A week after malik-malkin have gone, the blanket of melancholy enveloping Bhadoor gets mouldy. He won't move, he won't eat, he won't consider looking for other quarters. Fellow caretakers comfort him: "There are other kothis ... anyone will take an honest man like you." "We'll find you something, don't worry." "You have two adult sons. Let them look after you."

But Bhadoor is not asked to move out.

To the new malik-malkin who come to stay immediately after the old ones have left, he is like the moody water-pump that need not be replaced; like the repaired wall that protects and guards in spite of the scarred plaster, the memento of a drunken young man who had smashed his father's new car to its grave, and his, some years ago. He has been around before the faded, jaded, brittle moulded-plastic chairs that stand higgledy-piggledy on the terrace were bought. Like the crumbling, woebegone terracotta statue standing sentinel over the rusty pillar at the entrance, the righteous Bhadoor is an antique to be inherited. He gives the owners a sense of continuity, security, belonging.

"Goa's really different," the new malkin tells her friends. "The people are so-o nice. Our Bhadoor, for instance ..." Neither Bhadoor nor their house, their neighbourhood, their experience, is different from any in a colony in Noida or Aurangabad.

They have "fallen in like" with Goa because here they can wear loose blouses and shorts, drink without disapproving glances from in-laws, sleep late and be waited upon every waking minute of the day. Because it is a fashionable place to park one's money that knows no boundaries, moral, cultural or geographical.

The very day the new owners leave, Rajoo-Guddoo-Resham return.

"Bapuji," they excitedly tell Bhadoor, "There's so much happening in the markets. Let Hari get his brothers over. The vegetable-sellers need helpers. Here in the colony we get no news at all."

"Where will they stay?"

"People share huts. Share rents and save money."

Sundari wants her brothers to come, too. "But let them stay in quarters, not huts." She wants them to be, like Bhadoor, dependent on maliks for shelter, but not ghulams, no longer slaves to poverty.

Like in the ill-planned residential colonies sprouting around Coimbatore, Indore, Bangalore and Cuttack, so also in Dona Paula, opportunities favour the willing. Nameplates may change, but the houses stay put. As do the Bhadoors, the indispensable accessories that come with them.

"... where do you get servants like him nowadays?" New malkin, new terminology. The caretaker is dead. Long live the servant.

'Symbiosis' shared the third prize at the Fundação Oriente Short Story Competition 2011.

Cashew Nuts

Joaquim Dias

Cashew nuts sold at sixty rupees a kilo. That was a lot of money.

It was the summer holidays and Sanju was bored sitting at home. He had plenty of time on his hands. If he had that kind of money he could kill whole days. He could go to the movies, the beaches, and even to hotels. He lived in Khorlim, which was separated from Assagao by a small hill. And Assagao had huge cashew plantations.

The afternoon was the best time to steal cashew nuts. The *Kazkars* guarding the plantations mostly stayed at home to beat the heat, but a few kept vigil on random tree tops. Sanju had to be careful.

Once, he had been up on a tree, picking fruit, when a Kazkar caught him. He had not heard the man coming. He just had an eerie sensation of being watched and there was the man, shockingly right below him. It was too late to run. The man gently persuaded him to climb down, promising not to touch him. As soon as Sanju got down, the man caught him by the collar, emptied his pockets and slapped him.

"What's your name?"

"Sharad."

"Liar." Two slaps followed.

"Where do you stay?"

"Assagao."

"Liar." Two more slaps. And then, "How many times have you been here?"

It wasn't a question—it was an accusation. He just kept slapping Sanju around. Sanju's cheeks burned with shame.

"Go tell your folks you were beaten," he dared Sanju. "I'll be waiting for them."

Sanju told no one.

That was last year.

He had played that evening out in his head, recalling every slap and abuse in humiliating detail. At that time he had not known how to react. He picked his brothers' wallets regularly—but had never been caught. Or beaten.

Now, he wanted to get even. Besides, he could also have a little excitement and make a little money. But he would have to be careful.

First, he had to enlist the services of Eddie. Eddie went to school with him. He was one year his junior and two sizes smaller. He lived two houses down the road and sometimes, when no one was around, they sat in the backyard and smoked cigarettes. He wasn't exactly the partner Sanju had in mind, but Eddie was available. His mother worked in the Gulf and his father was hardly at home, so Eddie was free most times. Besides, Eddie was good at climbing trees.

He walked over to Eddie's house one afternoon.

"You won't believe this," he told Eddie, "there's a big car on the hill. Broken down. Jackie Shroff sitting inside. Let's go and see."

Eddie hardly ever went to the movies—his father forbade it. But he knew who Jackie Shroff was. He regularly visited the theatres after school, just to see the posters.

"Now?" Eddie asked.

"Yes now, Jackie's not going to wait for you. Let's move."

So Eddie locked the house, hid the key in the rafters and off they went in the blazing sun. It was a steep climb. Half way up, Eddie complained he should have brought his cap. A little further up the road, they could see the top of the hill, where the road crested before descending into Assagao.

There was no car in sight.

"It must be on the other side," Sanju said.

When they got to the top of the hill, the road was empty. Mapusa town baked in the distance to their left and to the right was the beaten green of scorched summer trees.

There was a small temple on the hill top where travellers and vehicles stopped to pray. Sanju removed his shoes, walked to the sanctum and said a prayer.

Later, they sat in the shade of the temple, discussing film stars. And all the while, Sanju watched the dull green expanse of cashew trees, flecked in turns by dots of red and yellow. The trees and the earth shimmered in the afternoon heat. It was a miracle that water could be found in this heat, sucked out from the dry earth and pushed up in the trees. He could even smell the high fruity reek of ripe cashews from that distance.

He looked carefully for movement—the shaking of trees, the presence and possibility of danger. Nothing moved. If he had to move, he had to move now.

"We're just sitting here, wasting time," Sanju said. "Let's get some cashews."

"Now?" Eddie asked.

"Now!"

There was an awkward silence between them. Sanju had made it sound casual, almost fun, but Eddie sensed things could go wrong. He had a vague idea he would be stealing and could get caught. But then, if he refused, he would be letting Sanju down. After having smoked all his cigarettes, it was hard to refuse Sanju, abandon him, and walk alone all the way home. That was treachery.

"What if there's trouble?"

"What trouble?" Sanju asked. "No trouble. I'm there, no?"

Eddie kept quiet. Sanju started walking towards the trees. Eddie quietly followed.

They walked into the plantation at a rapid pace, avoiding the beaten paths that zigzagged through the trees, and the clear spaces amongst them.

Eddie had another bout of misgivings: "What if there ...?"

"Shut up," Sanju whispered hotly in English, a finger on his lips. "No talking."

Sanju rarely used English and it had a startling effect. It shattered the illusion that they were just gallivanting. Eddie was now clear that the situation was dangerous.

Eddie loved crime and adventure and, in other circumstances, might even have enjoyed himself. He was a big fan of the Hardy Boys and Jupiter Jones. After school, when not staring at movie posters, he stalked the court and police station in Mapusa and got a thrill out of seeing handcuffed criminals being hauled in and out. He felt like a detective then.

But now, walking through the plantation, he felt like a rogue.

And then, just in case Eddie had any doubts left, Sanju asked him to climb a tree.

"What?" Eddie protested. "No way. I'm standing here only, I'm not climbing any tree."

But Eddie had to climb—it was best for them. He was thin and could go out on small branches. And trees didn't shake the way they did with Sanju's weight.

"I'll stand right here," Sanju promised. "Whatever happens, I won't move till you get down."

"Nothing doing."

They argued in hot whispers, till Sanju said, "Ok then, go back, pansy. I'll stay."

That did it. They were deep inside the plantation—no way was Eddie going back on his own.

"What if we get caught?"

"No one will get caught."

Eddie climbed the first tree tentatively. Then, having done it once, the others came easily, Eddie's confidence growing with every tree he climbed.

They moved to a plan. Sanju never carried the seeds on him. He hid them in small piles under fallen leaves. That way, if they were caught, there would be nothing on his person.

It was all over quickly—it took less than an hour.

They came out of the trees the same way they had entered, collecting their hidden piles along the way. And to Eddie's surprise, Sanju reached into his pants and pulled out a small cloth bag and began filling the seeds. It was clear that Sanju had set him up all along.

When they reached the temple, Eddie walked away.

That evening, Sanju went to see Eddie. He had sold the seeds at the Mapusa market. He tried to give Eddie ten rupees but Eddie refused to take the money.

The next day, Sanju suggested they go on an outing to a water spring. That seemed innocent enough and Eddie agreed. The spring was around eight kilometres away. They hired bicycles at fifty paise an hour and cycled there. Summer had reduced the stream to a mere trickle and they spent an hour in the water, jostling with other boys for space. They drove back wet, air drying as they cycled home. Sanju paid the bicycle man.

The following day, they went to Alankar theatre for a movie. That took a lot more convincing from Sanju. They sat in the front rows where the tickets were cheap at one rupee twenty paise and the eyes hurt from the glare. Sanju paid for the tickets and, in the interval, he bought boiled channa stuffed in slender paper cones. The last channas jammed at the bottom and Eddie retrieved them by tearing open the paper cone. All evening he had the nagging worry that someone might see him—then there would be trouble at home. But the evening went without incident.

Two days later, when Sanju suggested they take the bus to Anjuna, Eddie was incredulous. How was it possible to catch a bus, go to Anjuna, spend time there and get back home before eight o'clock? It was madness. But Sanju said he had done it before. And it was obvious that he had done it before, for he knew exactly where to go to catch the hippies naked. They laughed nervously at the naked bodies, their pleasure somehow reduced in each other's company. They ate channa, drank Limca and sat on the beach, tracing absurd figures in the sand with their fingers while they furtively watched the women. Then Sanju got bored. He walked over to a nearby shack and came back with a quarter of feni. He offered some to Eddie, but Eddie refused. So

Sanju drank the bottle and on the way back, with the exception of a slight slurring and red eyes, there was no way of knowing he had been drinking.

Sanju paid for everything.

In fact, Sanju had been paying for everything for over a week now. All this was more than what Eddie had expected for climbing a few trees. He had no idea how much money Sanju had made from the cashew nuts, but surely more than his share had been returned.

A few days later, Sanju surprised Eddie in the afternoon.

"Let's go see Jackie Shroff," he said. He had a big smile on his face.

"Right now?"

"Yeah, and don't wear a cap, and no chappals. Put on your tennis shoes."

They climbed up the hill and stopped at the temple. Sanju said his prayer.

This time they crossed the road to raid the plantations on the other side. This was more dangerous, for the hill fell sharply here and the houses of the Kazkars were even closer to the tree line. Escape would be harder. But it had to be done this way. Raiding the same place twice within a week would have been even more fraught with risk.

They sat at the edge of the plantation, watching the trees for movement. The trees here were thicker and darker and better loaded. They didn't start plucking with the nervous hurry that they were in the first time. They first marked out the better trees, systematically working them one after the other.

They spent, at most, an hour. And now Sanju pulled out two bags from his pants.

They filled the bags and didn't stop running till they

were clean past the road and on the other side of the hill, overlooking Mapusa town. They sat down on the rocks to rest.

That evening, Sanju called Eddie out on the road and stuffed twenty rupees in his pocket.

"Your money," Sanju said. "You earned it."

Later, Eddie pulled out the twenty rupee note and considered it. Twenty rupees was a lot of money. But he felt little pleasure. It felt wrong. He made a decision. He would go around with Sanju to the movies and cycling and whatever foolhardy idea he came up with—but he would not go in the trees again.

But then Eddie stopped going to the movies altogether. He almost got caught.

They had been to the cinema at Alankar theatre one evening. Coming out, Eddie almost ran into his father. Reacting quickly, he turned his face and dashed across the road to hide amidst the customers in the shops there. Worming his way through the crowd, he found himself standing at a counter. To his horror, he realised he was in a tavern. Drunk men stared at him; a bartender, glass in hand, waited for him to order. Meanwhile, his dad walked by, but Eddie didn't move till he had disappeared from sight.

That was close! If he had been caught, he would have got a thrashing.

After that, he decided, no more movies for him.

Instead, they would go cycling.

Every day, they gave themselves two hours. They started at five in the evening, cycling through unknown places until it was six. That was the cut-off point, when it was still light and they could still read the time easily on their cheap watches. Then they would turn back, before the light started to fade. They explored places and villages whose names they had never heard of and which they never knew existed. Sometimes, Sanju would stop at a roadside tavern, have a quick one and carry on.

Once, they had a good fright. They had cut into a bylane on the Siolim road, and when they returned, they realised they had missed a turn. There were no lights and they cycled by themselves on the narrow bumpy road. After a long time, they came across a man walking alone in the dark. His face glowed eerily from the beedi he smoked. He told them they were going in the right direction. They cycled on for a few kilometres more without seeing any light or movement. All they could hear were the chirping of crickets and other night sounds. Panic began to set in and they wondered if the old man had tricked them. They had been thinking of turning back when they saw the distant lights near St Xavier's College.

When Eddie got home, it was well past eight and his dad was waiting for him. He was livid. But he was praying and had a rosary in his hands. He could not really be violent in that piety.

"Your mother's slogging in the Gulf, and you're fooling around here?" his dad said. "Do you know how hard she works? Did you open your books today?"

He wanted Eddie to become a doctor.

"You cannot get up one day and say 'Ah now, I'll become a doctor', it doesn't work that way. You have to study every day, make the habit of studying right now."

Eddie's father had no education and no job but he saw nothing wrong in his demands.

Sanju had no such problems. No one wanted him to become a doctor, an engineer or anything like that. In fact, no one bothered with what he did. He had no parents and he lived with his elder brothers. The brothers were married and were busy with their wives and children.

The next day, Sanju was back, suggesting they go cycling through Parra.

"We'll be back in no time," he said. "I promise."

And he was right. They were back in no time.

But Sanju wasn't right every time.

They tried to enter the cashew plantations a third time. Eddie protested and argued and pleaded. But Sanju promised nothing would go wrong.

They almost got caught.

Hardly had they entered the trees when they heard the barking of dogs. They realised the dogs were on to them. It was only a short sprint to the safety of the road.

They stood there and waited.

Presently a man came out of the trees with a dog on a chain. Eddie walked away. Sanju didn't budge.

The man walked up to Sanju and stood at arm's length from him. They stared at each other. The dog growled on the chain. Eddie stopped in his tracks and watched them from a distance.

"I know you," the man said.

"Yeah," Sanju said, "I'm famous like that."

"You be careful, if I ever catch you there,"—the man waved his hands towards the trees—"you'll get it good."

"You can't do that here?"

"If I remember right, you found that out last year, didn't you?" the man taunted him. "Why don't you try again?"

The threat left hanging, the man quietly went back into the trees.

Later, Eddie wanted to know what happened.

"Nothing," said Sanju. "Just bullying. And never run like that—it makes you guilty."

But after that, they never went into the trees again.

The holidays were coming to an end and they had grown tired of cycling. They had cycled through every road that ran in and out of Khorlim. But there was still time to kill and now, instead of cycling, they began walking. They left their homes at five, climbed the hill and walked the main road to Assagao, surrounded by the very plantations they had robbed.

They sat at the edge of the road, smoked cigarettes, and waved at the hippies who sped by on their motorcycles.

One evening they were returning home and were on the Assagao side of the hill. It was the loneliest stretch of the road, where it curved sharply out of view. A motorcycle raced past them and at the curve, they heard a screech, followed by a crash.

For a long moment there was utter silence.

Then they heard the low moaning. They ran back down the hill. As they turned the curve, they saw the fallen motorcycle. The hippie riding it had fallen in the ditch. A woman had been flung face down on the road.

The moment the hippies saw them, they acted strangely. They picked themselves up quickly: the man kicking his bike furiously to start it; the woman limping back painfully. Before they had reached them, the hippies sped away. It seemed as though they were afraid of them. And Sanju felt they were trying to hide their faces.

They stood at the spot for a long time, examining the scratch marks of the bike, surprisingly white against the black road. There were oil stains and patches of blood. Then, in the ditch, Sanju saw a small box. It seemed like some kind of medical box. When they opened it, it was filled with syringes and needles.

Sanju wouldn't touch the box.

"You keep it," he said. "You're the one who's going to be a doctor."

He sounded cool but Eddie could sense the unease.

Sometimes, Eddie thought, it was strange what people got scared of.

Not Mum's Jaw

Fatima M Noronha

WAVES of heat, along with the Angelus peal, rolled over us, but no one stopped to pray. Namdev and Kistu wanted to finish the job by lunchtime. So did I. Sweat dripped off their chins. Their shorts covered with red dust, they shovelled out heap upon heap of loam. I coveted that mud, made of the goodness of human bodies. My chikku saplings longed for compost like that.

One of the handles of Dad's coffin slid down the pile. I picked it up. It was made from a biscuit tin. The other handles appeared in turn. Nothing else showed there had been a coffin here. I stood at the crater's edge, waiting. The diggers worked gently now, lifting off shallow layers of soft soil. When they found the remains, they brushed away the clods with their bare hands.

The skeleton in the blue-black suit lay as the body had lain twelve years earlier, precisely the way Dad used to sleep. That suit—he wore it to my wedding, to my middle sister's wedding in this very church, to my mother's funeral, and, shortly before he died, to my little sister's wedding. He wore the same dark tie, too, and I would not be surprised if it was the same white shirt every time. Whatever Dad could spare he gave to someone else.

"Do you want the skull?" asked Namdev, senior gravedigger at Saint Andrew's.

"Yes," I said. "Is there water in that tap to wash the bones?"

"No, *bai*, the tap stops by mid-morning. There is water in the open tank."

They did their work, moving the parts that had long been still. Gone was the mirage of a complete body. Shreds of blue-black fabric mingled with russet loam. The skeleton, now visible, was only the big sections really, no carpals, metacarpals and phalanges. Kistu shook the skull free, blew on it, and flicked a crust off the forehead. Bar me, no one ever presumed to flick a particle off my father's sleeve in his day.

Within minutes Kistu handed me the perfect skull and three long bones. He gathered the rest in his aluminium basin, which he emptied into the open ossuary—the Ezekiel Corner—at the edge of the cemetery. Waiting for him to return, Namdev lit his bidi and sat smoking on the nearest marble slab.

"Now you have to find my mother's bones. They were dug up on my father's funeral morning and buried in a suitcase at the head of his coffin."

"It's a wonder you knew where to look for your father," he said. "Even the headstone's been stolen. There's nothing to show it's a grave at all."

"Oh, I knew it was near the dentist's fancy vault over here."

In my youth I knew the dentist well enough, mildness itself when you met him in the street, but a terror with the forceps. We preferred to go to his rival, Muhammad Ali, despite the knock-out name. How often is a book like its cover?

Namdev was right about our family sepulchre. Archaeologists would probably not have found it. When Mum died, there was only standing room among the regular rows, so her resting place was dug in the odd space between the last row and the whitewashed cemetery wall. Four years later, in a thunderstorm, Dad's coffin was lowered into the same grave.

My sisters, not I, kept track of the spot. On All Souls' Day each year they covered the rectangle with marigold petals. They lit candles and said a prayer. Being a vegetarian, I have always taken a detached view of mortal remains. Maybe that is why it fell to me to oversee the exhumation of our parents' bones, to transfer them to a niche in the graveyard wall.

It was well past midday. The workers had begun to lose patience. They had to be careful, though, not to break any vestige of my mother's bones.

"Nothing here, bai," Namdev declared after a while.

"Arrey, dig deeper," I urged.

Kistu's shovel clinked against something. He bent down and sifted the mud through his fingers. He held his trophy aloft.

"Jawbone!" said Namdev, his own jaw slack.

His mate looked closely at it and gasped. He quickly handed it to me.

"This isn't my mother's jaw."

Kistu may have thought I was scolding him. He said, "Bai, there is nothing else left."

I sat heavily on the dentist's tomb. True, it was a long time since I had seen my pretty mother, but I was sure the object in my hand bore no resemblance to her petite, hyperactive jaw. It looked, as she herself would have said, like the jawbone of an ass.

"I have to go and sort this out. Please wash those three bones, Namdev, and wrap them in this cloth." I poked around in my bag. "No one will rob them from the open niche, will they?"

"Na, bai."

"Then keep them there. I'll bring the mason's boy tomorrow to fix the slab. Thank you both. Please take this." They wiped their hands on their shorts, and accepted their wages.

I stomped up to the parish office.

"Where's Father?" I asked the dormouse hunched over his empty teacup.

"The parish priest is out," he drawled. He looked up at my face and hastened to add, "But you may meet Father Nascimento, if you wish."

That was a stroke of luck. Padre Nascimento had at his fingertips the four hundred and forty years of Saint Andrew's Church and of our town of Vasco da Gama, once a jewel in Goa's crown.

The vicar's audience hall was empty. I walked across to his antique desk and deposited the muddy jawbone on it. Padre Nascimento walked in with a stoop more of courtesy than age.

"Good afternoon, Father."

"What a pleasant surprise!"

I glowered at the excavated specimen on the table. "Senhor Padre, might you be able to explain how the jawbone of an ass landed in my mother's grave?"

He chuckled. Then he said, "Sit down, anh, dear lady."

He examined the maxillary relic, pausing to note the one remaining tooth that certainly was not my mother's. He smiled, his apple-smooth cheeks colouring.

"Would you like a glass of water?"

"No, thank you, Father. You have a theory, I can see."

"Yes. Only a theory."

Leaning back in the vicar's carved mahogany chair, he spoke without hurry.

"In your dear parents' time, Sant' André had a temporary parishioner named Sacra Família: Holy Family, no less! I knew him from my childhood, in Saligão. There we used to call him Sacru, but one fine day he started calling himself Sacrula! Why?"

I took a deep breath. I was in no mood to be entertained.

"Because," he said with a grin, "he was in love with his neighbour Ursula. Sadly, she said no. Poor Sacrula became—how shall I say it, anh?—unconventional! He wore brown robes like a Franciscan, and gave pious orations wherever he went. At first he went round on a bicycle. Much later, towards the end of the Portuguese era, when he came to live in Vasco da Gama, he rode a pony."

I sighed. Father Nascimento looked amused, and raised a bony index finger as he went on. "He lived as a paying guest over there, on the main road, near the Pereiras' house. And he was quite a sight, riding down Avenida Craveiro Lopes—you know, Swatantra Path—all the way down to the *praça*. He used to stop in front of the main entrance to the Câmara Municipal, our municipality building, and make his speeches."

"Did my mother know him, Senhor Padre?"

"It is likely she knew him by sight at least. Sacrula was the only parishioner who owned a horse. It is even more likely he knew your dear mother. Maybe he was one of her silent admirers. Many people who never met her used to see her here in church. She was very active, I am told. I met her once. A very fine lady!"

He must have noticed my lack of enthusiasm. He studied my face. "You are a lot like her."

"Hm." People said the same old things.

"But I must tell you about Sacrula's pony. That creature was his best friend. He took good care of it. Even so, it fell ill and died. Poor fellow, he wept like the monsoons in July. He came here and pleaded with the vicar to let his friend be buried in the churchyard." I sat up. Behind the black-rimmed spectacles, Father Nascimento's eyes brightened. His cheeks turned pinker.

"'Bury a horse in holy ground? No, no!' said the vicar—at that time, Padre Pedro António, I think your grandfather was a good friend of his. So Sacrula dug a trench in the strip between the cemetery fence and the main road, and buried the pony there. He could see the spot from his window across the road. A couple of years later, the church's holdings were surveyed, and the vicar built a boundary wall according to official specifications, leaving only the required setback from the main road. The new wall brought the pony's unmarked grave into the cemetery, much to our Sacrula's delight. With each new coffin that went into the ground, the old boundary lines grew less distinct. By the time I was posted here, there was no sign of the old fence, although the sacristan told me about it, you know, this gentleman is almost eighty, he's seen a lot."

My hands were over my face, my elbows on the vicar's desk.

"My good lady, please don't be upset." I could not answer him.

"I'm sure the parish authorities meant no offence, but I suppose the pony's grave was hollowed out to accommodate your dear mother's coffin."

Giggles found their way out through every chink in my anger. Three hours in that griddle of a graveyard had melted away whatever poise I otherwise affected. I felt close to tears, but all I could do was laugh. When I stopped shaking, I stood up.

"Thank you very much, Senhor Padre."

"You are most kindly welcome." He nodded, smiling. "God bless you, anh!"

I snatched up the pony's bone. It left a little red mud on the mahogany. Brushing it off in three strokes, my hand looked like Mum's when she slapped crumbs off the dining table. The similarity irritated me. It alarmed me. Was there something brutal in my bones too?

Marching down the stairs and out, I thought it was just as well only a brute's bone was found in Mum's grave. If Kistu had exhumed her jawbone, I—ever the dutiful daughter—would of course have washed it, wrapped it in white muslin and placed it in the niche along with my father's skull and three long bones.

That delicate little jaw of hers pronounced words of wisdom and comfort to other people. They would not have believed her capable of even thinking the words she reserved for her children, words that dug a pit in our path, words that insisted on keeping us company years after her jaw was at rest.

The gravediggers were gone, but the cemetery gate was open. With a jawbone pointer to help me read names and dates, I sauntered between the rows of graves of people I had known or heard about—sweet Tessie here, my teacher's drunken husband there, eight Dutch aviators who crashed into the Dabolim hillock in 1959.

In an ancient Goan ritual, the *voiz*, or medicine man, burns a dummy of the cause of your trouble, and you are promptly cured. The poor pony had done me no wrong, but its relic came in handy. I judged my distance from the high whitewashed walls of the Ezekiel Corner. A bone dump would do for a *voiz*'s fire, I thought, as I took aim.